Lindsey swallowed, her heart banging out of rhythm. He was bending towards her, his blue eyes capturing hers with a magnetic pull. 'Dan...?'

'Don't talk.'

In an almost imperceptible movement he slid his hands beneath her elbows and they rose as one. Instantly Lindsey felt her nerve-ends tingling, her breathing grow uncomfortably tight. She lifted her head, searing his gaze with hers.

'I need to do this again...'

Dan reached up, sliding the tips of his fingers over her face, feeling the gentle throb of heat under her skin, the feminine, fragile line of her jaw. Even as his thumb lifted her chin his fingers were seeking her nape, drawing her to him.

He lowered his head slowly, giving her the chance to end it if that was what she wanted. But she didn't, and her mouth gave a tiny sigh of welcome as his lips brushed hers, settling over their softness.

Lindsey was drowning in feelings she hadn't experienced for the longest time. Dan's mouth on hers felt *right*, their kiss pure and perfect.

And she didn't let herself think for one second whether any of this was sensible or sure. She was ... at all, an... knowing ...

D1424532

3 0120 02708044 9

Dear Reader,

Thank you for waiting so patiently for my new story. This time we're back in Casualty, with Dante and Lindsey.

It's true that your soul-mate does not have to be perfect—just perfect for *you*. And I have to tell you that Dan took a bit of prodding to let his star shine in this story. His past failed relationship has left him wary of looking for love. He wears aloofness like a cloak. Then along comes Lindsey, my gorgeous heroine. Perceptive and smart, she sees a different Dan. She beguiles him, challenges him. Slowly Dan opens the doors to his heart. He tastes heaven with Lindsey. But his past keeps getting in the way. Lindsey puts him on notice and Dan realises he's been hovering in the shallows. Now he'll have to make the swim of his life or lose her.

I'm delighted to present for your reading enjoyment *Weekend with the Best Man*.

Leah x

WEEKEND WITH
THE BEST MAN

BY
LEAH MARTYN

MILLS &
BOON®

All rights reserved including the right of reproduction in whole
or in part in any form. This edition is published by arrangement with
Harlequin Books S.A.

This is a work of fiction. Names, characters, places, locations and
incidents are purely fictional and bear no relationship to any real
life individuals, living or dead, or to any actual places, business
establishments, locations, events or incidents. Any resemblance is
entirely coincidental.

This book is sold subject to the condition that it shall not, by way of
trade or otherwise, be lent, resold, hired out or otherwise circulated
without the prior consent of the publisher in any form of binding or
cover other than that in which it is published and without a similar
condition including this condition being imposed on the subsequent
purchaser.

® and TM are trademarks owned and used by the trademark owner
and/or its licensee. Trademarks marked with ® are registered with the
United Kingdom Patent Office and/or the Office for Harmonisation in
the Internal Market and in other countries.

Published in Great Britain 2016
By Mills & Boon, an imprint of HarperCollins*Publishers*
1 London Bridge Street, London, SE1 9GF

© 2016 Leah Martyn

ISBN: 978-0-263-92627-9

Our policy is to use papers that are natural, renewable and recyclable
products and made from wood grown in sustainable forests. The logging
and manufacturing processes conform to the legal environmental
regulations of the country of origin.

Printed and bound in Spain
by CPI, Barcelona

Leah Martyn is the author of a number of books published by Mills & Boon. She loves the realism of Medical Romance and bringing her characters to life. She also writes short fiction and the occasional piece for her local paper. Leah lives with her husband in Queensland, Australia. She enjoys country markets, Aussie barbecues, the haunting stillness of the bush in summer and spending time with the people she loves.

Books by Leah Martyn

Mills & Boon Medical Romance

The Doctor's Pregnancy Secret
Outback Doctor, English Bride
Wedding in Darling Downs
Daredevil and Dr Kate
Redeeming Dr Riccardi
Wedding at Sunday Creek

Visit the Author Profile page
at millsandboon.co.uk for more titles.

For BRISROM—Brisbane Romance Writers—
where it all began.
I hope you're all still out there. And still writing.

Praise for
Leah Martyn

'A sweet story about a single mother trying to juggle
kids and work… I highly recommend this book!'
—*Goodreads* on
Daredevil and Dr Kate

CHAPTER ONE

FRIDAY MORNING IN Casualty was the last place Senior Registrar Dan Rossi wanted to be.

And not with this patient—a seventeen-year-old drug-addicted youth. He'd arrested. And now the fight had begun to save his life. A life this skinny kid had valued so cheaply. How dared he?

Dan's thoughts turned dark. 'Start CPR!' He bit the words out as the team began the familiar routine, working in concert around the senior doctor, responding to his clipped orders.

Expectations rose and fell as they treated the patient. Rose and fell again. Dan glanced at the clock. They'd done all they could but he didn't want to call it. Not yet. Not today of all days. And not with this patient. What a waste of a young life. 'Ramp it up!'

He felt the sweat crawl down his back, his heart like a jackhammer against his ribs. He shouldn't be here. He'd lost his mental filter. Lost it.

Lost it. Lost it…

'OK, he's back.'

Thank God. Immediately, Dan's chest felt lighter as if a valve had just released the pressure building inside him. He woke as if from a nightmare.

'Pulse rate sixty,' Nurse Manager Lindsey Stewart relayed evenly. 'He's waking up.'

Yanking off his gloves, Dan aimed them at the bin, missing by a mile. 'Do what you have to do,' he said, his voice flat.

And walked out. Fast.

Lindsey's eyebrows hitched, her green gaze puzzled as she watched his exit.

'That was a bit odd back there,' Vanessa Cole, Lindsey's colleague, said, as they watched their patient being wheeled out to ICU. 'What's biting Rossi?'

'Something's certainly got him upset,' Lindsey agreed. 'Dan's usually very cool under pressure.'

'He hasn't been here long.' Vanessa shrugged. 'And we don't know much about him yet. Perhaps it's personal—girlfriend trouble?'

'Does he have a girlfriend?'

'Please!' Vanessa, who seemed to be at the sharp end of all the hospital gossip, gave an exaggerated eye-roll. 'With that dark, smouldering thing happening?'

'That's a bit simplistic,' Lindsey refuted. 'Dan Rossi is a senior doctor. He wouldn't bring that kind of stuff to work with him. I'd better try to speak to him. If it's a work-related matter, it'll need sorting.'

'Oh, Lins.' Vanessa's voice held exasperation as she pushed the privacy screen open. 'Don't start taking the flak for Rossi's dummy spit. We run—that is, *you* run an extremely efficient casualty department. It's my guess he'll take a long lunch and snap out of whatever's bugging him.'

Lindsey's instincts were not quite buying that scenario. She recognised mental stress when she saw it, and Dan Rossi had been far from his usual self since the beginning of the shift. She frowned a bit, wondering just where he'd fled to.

'Dan's usually pretty good to work with.'

* * *

Dan knew he'd been discourteous to the team but today, for very personal reasons, he'd had to get out.

Had to.

In a secluded part of the grounds he sank into a garden seat, taking a deep breath and letting it go. Every sensible cell in his brain told him he shouldn't have brought his personal problems to work today. In fact, he shouldn't have come to work at all. If he'd thought it through, he'd have taken a mental health day available to all staff. Instead, he'd come to work in an environment where emotions went from high to low in seconds.

He made a dismissive sound in his throat. Having to treat that last patient had been the trigger that had shot his ability to be objective all to hell.

Addiction. And a foolish boy, abusing his body with no conception of the amazing gift of life. A gift Dan's own babies had never had. No chance to draw one tiny lifesaving breath. Two perfect little girls.

It was two years ago today since he'd lost them.

At the memory, something inside him rose up then flattened out again, like a lone wave on the sea. The grief he felt was still all too real. Grief with nowhere to go.

A shiver went right through him and he realised he'd rushed outside without a jacket. Lifting his hands, he linked them at the back of his neck. He needed to get a grip. Once he'd got through today, he'd regroup again.

Flipping his mobile out of his pocket, he checked for messages and found one from his colleague and closest friend, Nathan Lyons. The text simply said: Grub?

In seconds, Dan had texted back.

Leo's in ten.

* * *

With things in Casualty more or less under control, Lindsey decided to take the early lunch. She needed to get her head together. In the staffroom she collected the minestrone she'd brought from home and reheated it in the microwave. Ignoring the chat going on around her, she took her soup to a table near the window and buried her head in a magazine.

Halfway through her meal she stopped and raised her head to look out of the window. She'd have to say something to Dan. She couldn't just pretend nothing had happened. But how to handle it?

It wasn't as though they had any kind of relationship outside the hospital. What did she really know about him anyway? She knew he'd worked in New York and, more recently, he'd left one of the big teaching hospitals in Sydney to come on staff here in this rural city of Hopeton. But beyond that? Except for the fact that Dan Rossi kept very much to himself—and *that* alone was an achievement in an environment where you were thrown together all the time—she knew next to nothing about his personal life. But she remembered his first day vividly.

She'd sneaked a quick peek at him as the team had assembled for the start of the shift. Her quick inventory had noted his hair was dark, very dark and cut short, his eyes holding a moody blueness, the shadows beneath so deep they might have been painted on. His shoulders under his pinstriped shirt were broad. She had taken a deep breath and let it go, realising as she'd done so that she'd been close enough to smell he'd been shower-fresh. In the close confines where they worked *that* mattered to Lindsey.

Then he'd caught her looking. And it was as if they'd shared a moment of honesty, a heartbeat of intimacy. His mouth had pulled tight then relaxed. He'd almost smiled. Almost but not quite.

And for what it was worth the vibe was still there between them. But it seemed to Lindsey that for every tiny bit of headway she made with Dan Rossi on a personal level, he took off like a world-class sprinter in the opposite direction.

She blew out a long breath of frustration, slamming her magazine shut as she got to her feet. Why was she even bothering to try to find out what made Dan Rossi tick? After her last boyfriend had cheated on her so spectacularly, she'd questioned her judgement about men. How did you work out which of them to trust and recognise those who were into game-playing? And right now, after the rotten morning they'd had, it was all too heavy to think about.

Leo's was five minutes away from the hospital, the unpretentious little café drawing the hospital staff like bees to puffy blossoms. Chef Leo Carroll kept his menu simple. And he'd done his market research, opening at six in the morning to accommodate the early shift who just wanted a coffee and a bacon roll. Lunch began at noon and lasted until three. Then Leo closed his doors, cleaned up and went to play guitar at a blues bar in town.

Dan settled into one of the comfortable side booths and stretched out his legs. Already he could feel the tension draining from him. Nathan's continued support had steadied him in ways that were incalculable. Dan recalled the day he'd flown into Sydney from the States. He'd been standing feeling a bit bemused in the passenger lounge, getting his bearings, when he'd heard his name called. He'd spun round and found himself looking into a familiar craggy face lit with a lopsided grin.

'Nate!'

Before Dan could react further, he'd been thumped across the back and enveloped in a bone-crunching hug that had almost undone him. 'Glad you made it back in one piece, dude,' Nathan had said gruffly.

Dan had swallowed. 'How did you know I'd be on this flight?'

'I have my ways.' Nathan had tapped the side of his nose. 'Now, come on, let's move it. I'm short-term parked and it's costing me a fortune.'

Dan had booked into a boutique hotel near the harbour, intending to stay there until he could find an apartment. As they'd driven, Nathan had asked, 'Do you have some work lined up?'

'Starting at St Vincent's in a week.'

'Still in Casualty?'

'It's what I do best. You still in Medical?'

'It's what *I* do best.' Nathan had shot him a glance. 'Uh—not going to see your folks, then?'

'Not yet.' His family lived in Melbourne and while he loved and respected them, he just wasn't up for receiving their sympathy all over again.

A beat of silence.

'I've met a girl.' Nathan's embarrassed laugh eased the fraught atmosphere.

Dan spun his friend an amused look. 'Serious?'

'Could be. Think so. She's a flight attendant. Samantha Kelly—Sami.'

'Get out of here!' Dan leaned across and fist-bumped his friend's upper arm. 'Tell me about her.'

'She's blonde.'

'Yeah?'

'Funny, sweet, smart...you know...'

'Yeah. And she's got you wrapped around her little finger. Nice one, mate. I hope it works out for you and Sami.'

'Uh—if it doesn't pan out for you in Sydney,' Nathan said carefully, 'you could come across the mountain to us at Hopeton District. Get some rural medicine under your belt. We're always looking for decently qualified MOs.'

'Mmm—maybe.' Dan gave a dry smile. Nathan went on to enthuse about the vibrant country city a couple of hours from Sydney across the Blue Mountains.

'And would you believe you can still fossick for gold around Hopeton?' Nathan concluded his sales pitch emphatically.

And six months later Dan had taken everything on board and made the move and now here they were, with Nathan's and Sami's wedding just a week away and *he* was Nathan's best man.

Dan looked at his watch just at the moment Nathan burst through the door.

'Sorry I'm a bit late,' he apologised, sliding his big frame onto the bench seat opposite. 'Would you believe I've just had to cannulate three old coots on the trot—no veins to speak of, dehydrated as hell. Why don't old people drink water, for God's sake?'

'Because it's a generational thing,' Dan said patiently. 'They drink tea. Probably have done so since they could hold a cup.' Dan turned his attention to the short menu. 'We need to get a wriggle on. What are you having?'

'If there's pasta of some description, I'm your man.'

'There is,' Dan said. 'And I'll have the steak pie.'

Leo was there in a flash to take their orders. 'Won't be long, Docs,' he promised, batting his way back through the swing doors to his kitchen.

Nathan sent a narrowed look at his friend. He was well aware of the significance of the day in Dan's life. 'How's it going?' he asked quietly.

Dan's mouth bunched into a tight moue. 'Getting there, as they say.'

Nathan wasn't so sure and he knew his friend well

enough to ask, 'It's got to be hard for Caroline as well. Have you tried contacting her again?'

'What would be the point? She couldn't wait to dump me and our marriage—such as it was.'

'Yeah—well.' Nathan decided it was time for some straight talking. 'I don't want to be brutal, but it was never going to work after the babies died, was it?'

'Probably not.' Dan frowned. 'But she wasn't even willing to try!'

Nathan shook his head. They'd had this conversation before—or one similar. 'Listen, Dan, I've known you for a thousand years. It's in your DNA to be decent and, to use a very old-fashioned word, honourable. But you and Caroline weren't in love and, believe me, that's the only reason you should get married. And stay married. For your own sanity, you can't keep second-guessing all the what-ifs.'

Dan knew what Nathan said made sense and, God knew, he'd tried to let it go. His mouth gave a wry twist. 'The last time I spoke to Caroline, she said she'd *moved on*.'

'Then maybe it's time you did as well,' Nathan said frankly. 'Hey!' He injected an air of enthusiasm around them and beat a little drum roll on the table. 'It's Friday and Sami's decided we need a night out. There's a new club in town. Why don't you join us?'

Dan's insides curled. He could think of nothing worse than tagging along with a completely loved-up pair like Nathan and Sami. 'Thanks, mate, but I'll be fine. You and your bride-to-be have better things to do—or you should have.'

'Speaking of brides…' Nathan picked up the pepper mill and spun it between his hands. 'Sami wants us to wear cummerbunds.'

Dan snorted. 'I'd rather shove my head in a bucket of prawns.' He took a mouthful of water, very carefully replacing the glass on its coaster. 'I'd probably walk through fire to save your butt, Nathan, but I am *not* wearing a cummerbund at your wedding.'

Nathan gave a bark of laughter and confided, 'Sami reckons it's *modern vintage.*'

Dan looked unimpressed. 'Tell her the menswear shop in Hopeton have never heard of cummerbunds, let alone stocked them.'

'She said she'd order them online—but don't panic.' Nathan held up a hand in a staying motion, deciding to let his friend off the hook. 'I've talked her out of it.'

'How?' Dan's interest picked up. From what he'd seen, Sami was one determined lady. In the nicest possible way, of course.

'I had a mental picture of us with bulging satin waistlines and fell about laughing. Sami wasn't amused. She wrestled me to the sofa and belted me with her slipper. Then she saw the funny side and laughed too.'

And then they'd probably gone to bed, Dan thought. It was great Nathan was so happy, so…loved. He deserved to be. Dan wondered how long it would be before he had someone special to call his own. Someone to love and who loved him back the same way. Unconditionally. *And that was what had been missing with Caroline.*

'So it's sorted, then?'

'It is. When are you coming up?'

'The day before, on the Friday, if that's OK?' The couple were being married in Sami's home village of Milldale, some thirty miles north of Hopeton. The wedding reception was to be held at Rosemount, one of the historic homes in the district that had been revamped into a functions venue.

'Friday's fine,' Nathan said. 'Sami's booked us into the local pub. My folks are staying there as well.'

'Your meals, gentlemen.' Leo slid plates the size of cartwheels down in front of them. 'Enjoy.'

'This looks good.' Nathan rubbed his hands in anticipation. 'Dig in.'

Halfway through their meal, Dan said, 'When is Sami leaving her job?'

'She has already. She's going to start up her own business here, a travel agency cum tourist thing. She's had mega hits on her website already.'

'That's fantastic. You're going to settle here in Hopeton, then?'

'Yep.' Nathan twirled a length of spaghetti around his fork. 'It's a good fit for us at the moment. And my job's safe—well, as far as any job can be these days.'

Dan's throat closed for a moment. Nathan's future seemed secure and...*good*. If only his own future had a semblance of the same simple expectations attached to it. He shook his head. God, he'd better lighten up, or he'd be like a wet blanket at his friend's wedding.

As if he'd tuned into Dan's thoughts, Nathan said, 'Have you written your best man's speech yet?'

'Not yet.'

'Don't say anything too incriminating that'll get me hanged, will you?'

Dan's mouth twitched. 'Like the after-rugby parties when we were at uni?'

'You were there too, matey,' Nathan reminded him. 'Let's not forget that.'

A swirl of emotions juxtaposed in Dan's head. They had been good times. Uncomplicated. Until *life* had happened. He swore inwardly. He had to release this choking collar of useless introspection. But it was the day, he justified. The date. The memories. 'I suppose I could talk about your peculiar eating habits.'

'Like what?' Nathan gave an offended snort.

'In all my travels, I've never seen anyone consume food as quickly as you.'

'It's a gift.' Nathan gave a Gallic shrug. 'What can I do?'

Dan chuckled. 'Ratbag.'

'So,' Nathan asked, suddenly serious, 'how was it this morning in A and E?'

'I wish you hadn't asked me that.'

'You didn't kill anyone, did you?'

Dan shook his head. 'Probably worse. I dumped all over the team in Resus and walked out.'

'Crikey. I'll bet Lindsey Stewart was impressed—not!'

Dan grimaced.

'Did you apologise?'

'Not yet.'

'Lins has the respect of the whole hospital.' Nathan looked serious. 'You'd better do a real grovel. Ask her for a drink after work and do it then. Properly.'

Dan felt worse and worse. He'd apologise, of course. But ask her for a drink? She'd probably turn him down flat. And he wouldn't blame her. In the short time he'd been at Hopeton he'd hardly put himself out to get to know her or anyone else. Out of nowhere, Lindsey Stewart's flashing green eyes seemed to challenge him. And he realised on some basic level that he *wanted* to get to know her. To break away from the past. He had to turn things around. 'I shouldn't have come to work today.'

'Possibly not,' Nathan agreed. 'Just fix it, mate. Hopeton's not so big that bad behaviour goes unnoticed.'

CHAPTER TWO

BACK AT THE STATION, Lindsey glanced at the clock and sighed. She couldn't wait for the shift to end. And thank heaven she had some leave coming up. And where was Dan? She scanned the precincts with a practised eye. Probably, as Vanessa had supposed, enjoying a long lunch. Except he wasn't late back, she admitted fairly. It was her own fault she'd taken only the briefest lunch break. But she'd got sick of her own company and her mixed-up thoughts had been driving her nuts. She needed to be busy.

Dan made his way slowly towards the station. There she was, sitting with her back towards him, her dark head with its subtle streaks of auburn bent over some paperwork. He silently thanked all the gods she was on her own. He couldn't do this in front of an audience. His breathing faltered, his stomach churned and he went forward. 'Lindsey…'

She spun round and looked up. 'Dan…'

Dan rubbed at the back of his neck, feeling his muscles bunch but not release.

For a few seconds there was an awkward silence as they both took stock.

'I owe you an apology,' Dan said eventually.

Lindsey stood up. She'd feel better able to sort this standing eye to eye. She sent him a cool look. 'Do you have a problem with the nursing back-up in the department? Or a problem with me?'

'Of course I don't.' Dan felt a spark of anger. Where had she got that idea? He gave a tight shrug. 'I was out of line earlier. I'm sorry. It won't happen again.'

Lindsey felt her whole bearing soften. His ownership of his lapse was more, much more than she'd expected. She lifted her chin and met his gaze, suddenly aware they were close, too close for comfort. What was he thinking? She couldn't tell. His eyes were clouded with uncertainty. Out of nowhere, Lindsey felt a twist of uncertainty herself. She hated being out of sync with any of her colleagues. Hated it. 'Stuff happens in Casualty.' She gave an open-handed shrug. 'Don't beat yourself up.'

'Thank you.' Dan felt the ton weight lift from him. He gave a tight smile. 'Put it down to an off day. We all have them, don't you agree?'

'I guess we do,' Lindsey said carefully. And if she was any judge of the human condition, he was still having an off day. He seemed a bit...*desperate*, for want of a better word. Edgy. And there were shadows beneath his eyes. Again. If anyone needed a hug, it was Dan Rossi. But that would be totally out of order. Unprofessional. And embarrass the socks off him. She looked away quickly. In seconds, the tenor of her day had changed completely. What was going on here had no rhyme nor reason. It was just... happening. And she felt she was jumping fences ten feet high and couldn't stop. It was an extraordinary sensation.

Dan swallowed through a very dry throat. She had her hair twisted into a topknot and flyaway strands were coming loose. He wondered what it would look like if she were to let it tumble down, releasing the scent of the flowery shampoo she used. It wasn't going to happen. In an almost reflex action she reached up, pushing the wayward strands back in. Dan fisted his hands, resisting the urge to do it for her. 'So, what's on the agenda?'

Lindsey put her nurse's head on quickly. 'We have a little kid waiting for sutures. Michelle and Andrew are presently treating a youth with burns, the result of walking barefoot on coals after a bush barbecue. If you'd rather take over there and have one of them see the child…?'

'No, no.' Dan frowned a bit. 'Our junior doctors need to gather experience. I'll see the child. Point me in the right direction.'

'I'll come with you,' she said, as Vanessa took over the station.

'Fill me in,' he said, as they walked towards the cubicles.

'Preschooler, Michael Woods. He was chasing a ball out of bounds, tripped and hit his chin on the edge of a brick garden bed. Fair bit of blood. Panic stations and the school rang mum. She's with him.'

'Good. She'll be a calming influence.'

Lindsey chuckled. 'You hope.'

'Are you saying it's the mothers we have to be afraid of, Lindsey?'

Lindsey turned her head and caught his gaze. She blinked a bit. Unless she was mistaken, there was actually a curve happening to one corner of his mouth. On impulse, she sent him a full-blown smile in return, urged on by a feeling of oneness with him she couldn't explain. 'I've met a few.'

Five-year-old Michael was sitting on the edge of the treatment couch, his small legs swinging rhythmically back and forth. He didn't look overly upset, Lindsey noted thankfully, although the blotches of dried blood on his T-shirt indicated it had been a heavy bump to his chin.

Dan smiled at the mother. 'Mrs Woods? I'm Dan Rossi. I'll be the doctor looking after Michael.'

'I'm Stephanie.' Michael's mother kept her arm protectively around her little boy's shoulders. She gave a wry smile. 'He's a bit of a tornado in the playground.'

'So, you like playing footy, Michael?' Dan asked.

'I can kick the ball as high as the house,' Michael declared, aiming upwards with one small arm.

'Fantastic.' Dan looked impressed.

Lindsey gave him a tick of approval for keeping things light and thereby gaining their small patient's trust. Unobtrusively, she gloved and said quietly, 'I'll pop that sticking plaster off Michael's chin, shall I, Dr Dan?'

'Let's do that.' Almost casually, Dan hooked over a mobile stool and snapped on gloves. He sat in front of Michael. His eyes narrowed slightly. The removal of the plaster had revealed a gaping hole underneath. The mother's gasp was audible. 'Easily fixed.' Dan's tone was gently reassuring. Tilting Michael's chin, he examined the damage more closely. The edges of the wound were uniform. They would align nicely. It would be a neat scar.

'Is he OK?' Stephanie asked anxiously.

'His bite seems even,' Dan responded. 'And his baby teeth all seem in place. I'll put a stitch or two in his chin and he should be as right as rain.'

Gently, Lindsey positioned Michael for the suturing procedure, laying him back with his head at the end of the bed.

Dan rolled across the trolley containing the instruments he'd need and switched on an overhead light. 'Now, Michael, this is where you have to be as brave as the best footy player in the world,' Dan said, flicking up the syringe of local anaesthetic.

Michael's blue eyes lit up. 'Like David Beckham.'

Dan huffed a laugh. 'That's the guy. Now, if you lie very still for me while I make your chin better, I'm sure

I can find an amazing sticker you can wear on your shirt tomorrow and show the kids at preschool.'

'My shirt's all dirty,' Michael said with childish logic.

'Honey, we'll find you a clean one to wear.' Stephanie smiled at her son and held his hand tightly.

Dan looked up. 'Lindsey, if you would, please?'

She nodded. The injection of the lignocaine would sting and be a shock to the little one. 'Squeeze Mummy's hand hard, Michael,' she said, placing herself gently across the child's body in case he tried to wriggle free.

In a few seconds the local had been injected and they waited a couple of minutes for it to take effect. Dan prodded the wound gently in several places. 'Can you feel anything hurting, Michael?'

Eyes squeezed shut, Michael said, 'No…'

'Good boy. Keep holding Mummy's hand and we'll be finished in no time.'

In a short time Lindsey watched Dan snip the last suture close to the skin. 'There you are, sweetheart.' She gave the little shoulder a gentle pat. 'All finished.'

'Can I get my sticker now?'

Dan looked a question. He'd promised one to his small patient. He just hoped they had some in the department.

'They're in a box at the station,' Lindsey said right on cue. 'Won't be a tick.'

'Gorgeous little boy, wasn't he?' Lindsey remarked lightly as she went about tidying the treatment room.

Dan was parked at the mobile tray, writing up his notes. He lifted his head in query. 'Sorry?'

'Michael,' Lindsey said. 'He'll probably be a real heartbreaker.'

'Yes, probably…' Dan went back to his notes, finishing them swiftly.

'Thanks.' He gave the ghost of a smile and left quietly.

Lindsey bundled the soiled linen into a bin with a vengeance. What was with this guy? Would it kill him to indulge in a bit of normal conversation?

Dan was amazed how quickly the rest of the shift passed. The ache in his shoulders had disappeared. Cautiously, he began to feel, as a result of the sudden turnaround with Lindsey, he might have a chance at some kind of normal life here at Hopeton. A chance he couldn't afford to ignore.

Deep in thought, he began collating paperwork at the station. There were some end-of-shift letters he needed to write to several GPs. In Dan's opinion, their respective patients would need referral—

'Still at it?' Lindsey stopped at the station, her brows raised in query.

Dan's mouth tipped into a rueful smile. 'Still a bit of tidying up to do. You're off, then?' His fingers curled round his pen. Idiot. It was the end of her shift. Of course she was *off.* Gone were the hospital scrubs; instead, she was wearing soft jeans that clung to her legs and a long-sleeved silver-grey top, a silky scarf in a swirl of multi-colours around her throat.

And knee-high boots.

Dan felt his heart walk a few flights of stairs. He couldn't think of a single thing to say to the beautiful woman standing in front of him. And how pathetic was that?

'It's Friday, you should give yourself an early mark.' Lindsey looked more keenly at him. The lines of strain were still there around his eyes. He needed to relax. But whether or not he'd allow her to help him do that was another matter entirely.

But for some reason she couldn't fathom, she had to try. 'Most of us are going to the pub. Few drinks, a game of snooker, a pizza or five later. You're very welcome to join us.'

Dan's heart suddenly came to a halt. *Thank you, God.* 'Sounds good. Uh—which pub?'

'The Peach Tree. Ancient red-brick place at the top of the main street. See you there, then?'

'You bet.' He nodded enthusiastically. 'Thanks for the invite.'

'Welcome.' Lindsey hitched up her shoulder bag and turned, moving off quickly to catch up with Vanessa.

A fleeting frown touched Dan's eyes as he watched the two women make their way towards the exit. He took a long controlling breath and let it go. Thanks to Lindsey's invitation, he'd taken the first steps towards his new life.

With the thought still humming in his head, he went back to his office to type up his referrals.

Letters completed, Dan swung up from his desk, looking up in question when Martin Lorimer, the senior doctor on take, poked his head in. 'Ah—Dan. You're still here. MVA coming in. Pile-up on the highway, two vehicles, all teenagers. Can you hang about?'

Dan felt his gut contract. Did he have a choice? *Hell.* Lindsey would think he'd bottled out or just been plain rude. And he didn't need that kind of misunderstanding after today's debacle. He'd text her if he could but he had no idea of her mobile number. He swore under his breath. If the injuries to the kids were not too serious, maybe he'd still make it to the pub. Holding that thought, he made his way towards the ambulance bay.

'I got you another OJ.' Vanessa placed the glass of juice in front of Lindsey. 'And what's with you tonight, Lins? We could have won the snooker if you hadn't been so not into it. Now I owe Andrew ten bucks.' Vanessa pleated a

strand of her blunt-cut blonde hair behind her ear. 'Um…
do you think Andrew might be a bit keen?'

'On you?' Lindsey took a mouthful of her drink.
'Maybe. Every time he needs a hand with a patient, he
makes a beeline for you.'

'So, do you think he's ever going to get off his butt and
do something about it?'

'Why wait for him? Van, you live in the same building.
Surely you run into him about the place. Just ask him in
for a coffee or something.'

'But if he said no, I'd feel stupid,' Vanessa moaned.
'And I have to work with him.' She ran her finger around
the rim of her glass. 'Did he seem to miss me while I was
on leave?'

'Not that I noticed,' Lindsey said drily. 'But he's coming over now. Perhaps you're about to find out.'

'You bet I will.' Full of resolve, Vanessa whirled to her
feet. 'Are you off home?' She gave Andrew a pert look
and a very warm smile.

'Think I'd better. I'm back on a late tomorrow.'

'Oh, me too.' Vanessa grabbed her bag. 'Let's share
a cab. I'll put the ten bucks I owe you towards the fare.
Deal?'

'Deal.' Andrew's white smile gleamed. The two took a
few steps away then turned and chorused, ''Night, Lins.'

Lindsey dredged up a smile and fluttered a wave. Ten
minutes later her eyes did another tour of the lounge. Still
no Dan. Inwardly, she gave a philosophic little shrug. She'd
invited him and he hadn't shown. And yet he'd seemed
keen enough. Perhaps he'd thought better of it. Her mouth
turned down. And perhaps she'd come across as being too
pushy. Well, whatever, she wasn't going to hang about,
wondering.

Outside, the night was clear and crisp. Lindsey looked

up. The moon looked so pretty, hanging there like…a silvery seahorse…

'Lindsey!'

She spun round. She'd know that voice anywhere. Her heart jagged into overdrive. 'Dan?'

Dan emerged out of the shadows and into the filtered lighting at the pub's perimeter. 'You waited,' he said, and looked at her. 'I got caught up.' Briefly he filled her in.

'When will kids realise speed can be a potential killer?' Lindsey shook her head. 'They'll all be OK, though?'

'Should be, in time,' Dan replied, fisting his hands into the side pockets of his bomber jacket. 'I'm whacked,' he admitted frankly. 'Are they still serving meals here?'

'Long finished,' Lindsey said. 'The club scene's taken over now.'

'Uh, OK. Thanks for hanging about,' he said, hunching his shoulders in a shrug. 'I thought my not turning up might have ticked you off. I didn't want that.'

'I guessed you'd had an emergency,' Lindsey said, forgiving herself the small untruth. 'It's a bummer when that happens right at the end of a shift, isn't it?'

His blue eyes regarded her levelly. 'Well, this time it certainly was. I had no way of letting you know.'

Lindsey flipped a hand dismissively. 'We can fix that now, if you like.' She reached into her bag and pulled out her mobile and in a few seconds they'd exchanged numbers.

'So, we're good, then?' Dan's head came up in query and he returned his phone to his back pocket.

Lindsey swallowed unevenly. Running into him like this had been unexpected. And now it all seemed a bit surreal. And why on earth were they standing here? It was freezing. 'What are you going to do about some food?'

'I'm sure I'll find somewhere to get a takeaway if I look hard enough.'

Lindsey bit the edge of her bottom lip. She had the sudden vision of him going back to his place, sitting alone, eating alone. After the kind of brutal day he'd appeared to have had, the mental picture was awful. The fact that it bothered her so much took her by surprise. She lived only a few minutes away. She could offer to feed him. An invitation hovered on the tip of her tongue...

'Do you have the weekend off?' Dan asked.

Lindsey snapped her thoughts back to reality. 'Yes. You?'

'Back on an early tomorrow.'

Lindsey made a face. 'Make sure you eat, then.' She cringed inwardly. She'd sounded like his grandmother.

'Thanks for caring.' His eyes held a penetratingly blue honesty.

'Mmm...' Lindsey's mouth went dry.

'I haven't exactly been fun to work with.' Half turning, he dragged a hand through his hair, leaving a few dark strands drifting across his forehead. It gave him a faintly dissolute air.

Lindsey scrunched her fingers through the folds of her scarf, suddenly shaken by the intensity of emotion that just standing next to Dan generated throughout her entire body. 'Maybe we should appoint a laughter coach for the ED.'

Dan felt disconcerted for a second. Her mouth was smiling. Just. More a tiny upward flick at the corners. He smiled back and, for just a moment, a blink of time, there was a connection of shared awareness. Sharp. Intense. And then it was gone, retracting like the sun under cloud. 'Take that idea to the board.'

'Would I have your backing?'

Was she serious? 'You bet. Laughter in the ED sounds... remedial.' And ridiculous. In fact, the whole conversation was verging on the ridiculous. Which only went to prove how out of touch he was with the ordinary stuff, like social interaction. Especially with beautiful women. The atmosphere was fraught again.

'If you're looking for a takeaway, the Chinese should still be open,' Lindsey offered.

He gave a one-shouldered shrug, moving restively as though he wanted to be away. 'Maybe I won't bother after all. I've food at home. I can whip up something.' *Or I could ask you to come and have a coffee with me.* His thoughts churned with indecision. He took the easy way out and said, 'You're OK getting home, then?'

'I'm parked just over there.' Lindsey indicated the small sedan the same make as a dozen others in the car park. 'Where are you?'

'Near the exit.'

Lindsey burrowed her chin more deeply into the roll collar of her fleece. This was bordering on crazy, standing here like two puppets waiting for someone to pull their strings and activate their mouths. She felt like chucking all her doubts and insisting he come home with her for a meal. Instead, she lowered her head and began fishing for her car keys in her bag.

Dan's jaw tightened as her hair fell forward in a shimmering curtain and it was all he could do not to reach out and draw it back and hold it while he pressed a slow, lingering kiss on her mouth...

'Got them.' Lindsey held up the keys triumphantly. Her gaze held his for a long moment. Expectant. Something... 'I guess I'll see you at work, then.'

Dan managed a nod. Whatever chance he'd had to further their...*friendship* outside the hospital had gone now. He'd stuffed it. 'Guess so.'

'Make sure you eat,' she reinforced, and they both took off in different directions.

'Hey, Lindsey!'

She turned. He was walking backwards and smiling. 'In case you were wondering, I *can* cook.'

'Never doubted it.' Lindsey's own smile carried her all the way home.

Wednesday, the following week...

'Told you he'd shape up.' Vanessa's voice held vindication, as they completed handover for the late shift.

'Andrew?' Lindsey feigned mild interest.

Vanessa gave an eye-roll. 'Our Dr Rossi. He's been exceptionally co-operative and I detected quite a nice sense of humour lurking somewhere there.'

'I've hardly seen him this week.' Lindsey made a pretence of checking the list of patients waiting in cubicles. 'His shifts have obviously been all over the place.' And she'd noticed his absence. Oh, boy, had she noticed.

'Well, if you're happy with everything, I'm out of here.' Vanessa hauled off her lanyard and scattered a handful of pens into a nearby tray. 'Andrew and I are going to a movie.'

'Well, fancy that...' Lindsey drawled. 'He's finally asked you out on a date.'

'Well, actually, I asked him. But he was all for it,' Vanessa added quickly.

'Good for you, Van.'

'Well, the opportunity kind of just presented itself,' Vanessa said modestly. 'But it just goes to show, doesn't it? Some men merely need a shove in the right direction.'

Was there a message somewhere in there for her? Lindsey's eyes were thoughtful as she set about triaging the patients on her list.

CHAPTER THREE

LINDSEY TURNED UP the music and did a rhythmic little rock with her shoulders as she drove. It was Friday at last and she was on leave. *Going home*. It was a good feeling. And perhaps back among the vines and the majestic blue hills she'd be able to sort out her feelings about a certain doctor. Was she wasting her time, though? Maybe. Maybe not.

She shut her music off. It was time to concentrate on her driving. Even though the country road was bitumen and usually well maintained, it was narrow. And it was just on dusk, visibility questionable to say the least, but she hadn't wanted to hang about in Hopeton. With the thought of home beckoning, she'd just wanted to be on her way.

Automatically, she concentrated her vision on the road ahead. The headlights of an approaching car were illuminating the horizon. Lindsey adjusted her own headlights in preparation. She noticed there was a vehicle behind her as well. But so far it was obeying the road rules and keeping a safe distance.

Dan's thoughts were very mixed as he drove. He hadn't managed to catch Lindsey much over the past week. And that had been a frustration. He'd wanted to reinforce the little progress he'd made in getting to know her. But his hours at work had been manic, only because he'd made himself available so as to accumulate a few days' leave after the wedding. The wedding was tomorrow. He hadn't prepared a speech so he'd speak off the cuff. He and Nathan had so much shared history, it shouldn't be difficult.

Abruptly, Dan was jolted out of his thoughts of weddings and speeches as he noticed the lurching drift of an oncoming car. *What the hell?* All his reflexes sprang into action. He reduced speed instantly, preparing to brake. For a split second he forgot to breathe, following the speeding car's trajectory as it plunged out of control, crossing the centre line and placing it on a collision course with the car in front of him. He felt every nerve in his body tense.

Surely, a crash was inevitable.

Lindsey hissed an expletive, all her defensive driver training coming into play. This couldn't be happening! Who was this lunatic of a driver? Her heart pounded, echoing in her ears. *Please, no!* She pulled hard on the steering wheel, feeling she'd dodged a bullet as the sports car shot past in a blur. She was safe. The relief was instant but short-lived as the vehicle clipped the rear section of her car, pushing her off the road. Her head snapped forward and then back, slamming into her headrest as her car spun and spun again.

Dan's jaw went rigid. This was a nightmare. He watched in horror as the sports car rolled before coming to rest right side up in a mangled mess of metal and broken glass. One headlight remained working, shining brokenly on the prostrate figure lying in the middle of the road.

It took a few seconds for the nurse in Lindsey to react. All thoughts of her own welfare fled. Pushing out of the car, she set her feet on the road. She felt woozy as she stood, swallowing back sudden nausea. She had to get to the injured person. She began running.

* * *

The sight of the female figure running towards the accident wrenched Dan out of his quagmire of disbelief. He brought his Land Rover as near as was safe to the accident site, switching his headlights to high beam. In seconds, he'd lodged a call for an ambulance. Seconds after that, he was out and grabbing his medical case, complete with oxygen and suction. He had a feeling he was going to need every last item in his kit. He took off at a run, noting the woman was already at the scene, crouching over the injured man. Dan frowned. Should she even be there? He'd seen how her vehicle had copped the impact of the sports car. 'Are you hurt?'

Lindsey startled at the brisk demand, raising her head. She blinked uncomprehendingly. 'Dan…?'

Sweet God. Dan let his breath go in a stream. 'Lindsey?'

For a mini-second they stared at each other in amazement and total disbelief. But the whys and wherefores had to wait until later. They had a life to save. 'Are you OK?' Dan rapped.

She frowned slightly. 'Think so…'

'Then let's see what's going on.'

The injured man looked in his sixties. Possible causes for the accident ran through Dan's head. Had he fallen asleep? Suffered a stroke or heart attack…? He was wearing bike shorts, T-shirt and hiking boots. Dan threw open his medical kit, snapping on a pair of gloves. Who was this guy—some kind of fitness nut? First things first, he decided, placing an oxygen mask over the man's face.

Lindsey hunkered down beside Dan. 'Ambulance coming?'

'Yep. They've diverted one. Let's hope it gets here in time.' Dan shook his head at the carnage. 'Glove up, please, Lindsey. I need your help here.'

She swayed a little then gathered herself, taking a deep

breath and then another, pulling on her gloves over shaking hands. 'Is he still breathing?'

'Just. Obviously he wasn't wearing a seat belt to be thrown out like that.' Dan did a quick head-to-toe check. 'Multiple contusions, by the look of it, fractured tibias.' He ripped out an expletive. 'Arterial bleed from his groin.'

Lindsey felt her stomach turn upside down, the sight of bright blood pulsing from the femoral artery almost making her gag. She took quick, shallow breaths, swallowing down the bitter taste of bile. Working like a robot, she grabbed whatever she could find in Dan's bag to absorb the flow of blood and pressed hard against the site. Pressure. They needed pressure. A tourniquet. An ambulance. A and E back-up. Her brain fogged. This was bordering on her worst nightmare. She'd attended dozens of accident scenes. What on earth was wrong with her…?

'Sure you're OK?'

Suddenly Dan was butted up against her. Lindsey felt the warmth of his hand anchoring hers. Her teeth began to chatter. 'Bit s-sick…'

'You're in shock!' God, why hadn't he noticed?

'I'll…be all right.' Lindsey forced herself to slow her breathing. In and out.

Dan scanned her face. Even in the dim light he could see she was as pale as parchment. 'Do you hurt anywhere? Lindsey, I need to know.'

She shook her head and winced as a spasm in her neck caught her unawares. 'Bit of…whiplash. I'll be OK. Just… get on.'

Dan hissed a non-reply. Within seconds, he'd wound a tourniquet into place.

Freed from the task of providing pressure on the wound, Lindsey pulled back. 'Do you have a collar?'

'No, damn it.' He shook his head at his lapse. Made a mental note to include one in his kit ASAP. 'We've got to stop that racket somehow,' he grated. They both knew their patient's airway was seriously compromised, his tortured breathing rattling into the stillness. He'd have to improvise. Dan's responses were running at top speed. He moved forward, kneeling so that the injured man's head was between his thighs. It was the only kind of stability he could offer for his patient's head and neck. Using gentle pressure, he extended the chin. The man's breathing improved marginally. It had to be enough until the paramedics got there.

Lindsey rallied, giving Dan the back-up he needed. She passed him the portable suction unit, automatically pushing the mask aside so he could place the sucker inside their patient's mouth. She felt black nausea pool in her stomach as blood tracked down into the tubing. Turning away, she retched onto the road.

'That's enough, Lindsey,' Dan ordered. 'I can manage from here.' He motioned backwards with his head. 'Go and sit in my car and wait for me. There's bottled water in an Esky on the floor. Drink.'

Wrapping her arms tightly over her stomach, Lindsey walked a bit unsteadily to the Land Rover. Opening the passenger door, she stopped, breathing away the coil of utter wretchedness. The few seconds' hiatus gave her some relief and she scrambled inside. Letting her head rest back, she closed her eyes and steadied her breathing.

It took only a few minutes for her stomach to settle. Feeling more in control, she leaned down and took a bottle of water from the Esky. She began sipping, feeling better after each mouthful. But now she was beginning to feel cold.

Dan's jacket was draped across the back of the driver's seat. Guardedly, aware she could overstretch her already sore neck muscles, she reached over and slowly managed to unhook the coat, draping it across her body like a blanket.

She felt herself relax, snuggling into its warmth, breathing in the faint scent of sandalwood and seasoned leather.

And him.

Out of nowhere, Lindsey felt a warm sensation down low, sensual tentacles humming through her whole body. She burrowed more deeply into Dan's coat. And felt connected to him in a way she could have only imagined.

Her mind flew ahead to something much more intimate and she snuggled deeper, as though taking his body warmth into herself.

Gradually, she became aware that the ambulance had arrived in a blaze of lights and a blaring siren, the police vehicle and a tow truck not far behind, the multi-coloured strobes looking like a weird kind of stage show. Lindsey watched through the windscreen, glad to be away from it all. Her tummy had settled but the feeling of it all happening to someone else persisted. Unfortunately, the reality was there in the ache of her neck muscles.

She could only hope the injured man would recover. And if he did, it was all down to Dan's skill as a doctor. He had been amazing.

Twenty minutes later the ambulance had gone. Lindsey registered the activity up ahead. The police had redirected the oncoming traffic. She wondered why there seemed quite a bit for this rather quiet road. But, then, it was Friday and lots of folk liked to get away for the weekend for wine tours and the B&B comfort offered by several of the vineyards around Milldale.

'How're you doing?'

Lindsey startled. The driver's door had swung open and Dan was there beside her. 'Much better.' She gave a wan smile. 'I borrowed your coat.'

'Good. I'm glad you had the sense to keep warm.' He sent her a perceptive look. 'I take it Milldale doesn't have a hospital?'

'Not even a GP. Why?'

'Why?' Dan frowned. 'Because I think I should take you straight back to Hopeton and get your neck X-rayed.'

'Oh, Dan...please, no.' Lindsey squeezed her eyes tightly shut in rebuttal. 'I'll be fine, honestly.'

'You can't know that for sure, Lindsey.' He seemed unconvinced. 'But I had a feeling you'd be stubborn so I managed to snaffle a collar from the paramedics.'

'No collars.' Lindsey was adamant. 'Look, it's whiplash, resulting in a bit of muscle strain. I have some massage oil that works miracles. I'll attend to it the minute I get to where I'm going.'

Dan quirked a brow. 'And where is that?'

'Milldale. Home.'

'Home,' Dan repeated. 'I thought you lived in Hopeton.'

'I do, for work. But home for me is Lark Hill, the vineyard where my parents live. Where I grew up. I'm starting a bit of leave.'

It took Dan only a few seconds to process all this. She still had some way to drive to Milldale before she could get relief for her neck pain. Was she fit to drive? Was her car even drivable? He came to a decision. He was a doctor, for God's sake. He could treat her. Here and now. 'Do you have your *miracle* oil with you?'

Lindsey looked uncertain. 'Of course I have it with me.'

'In your luggage?' Dan was slowly opening the driver's door. 'Tell me where to look and I'll massage it in for you. The sooner it's done, the sooner some relief will kick in for you.'

Lindsey's hands clutched the collar of his coat, pulling it higher as if to ward off the idea. She couldn't let him do that. It was too intimate...too...everything. She moistened her lips. 'If you get me the oil, I can rub it on myself.'

He snorted. 'And how high can you lift your arms without it hurting?'

Emotions began clogging Lindsey's throat. If she was honest, she was aching all over and suffering the aftermath of shock. It would be so lovely to let go of all her scruples and let Dan take care of her. 'My car keys are still in the ignition.'

'And your luggage in the boot?' Dan swung one leg out of the car.

Lindsey managed a small nod. 'Just bring my beauty case. It's black with—'

'Lindsey, relax,' Dan broke in gently. 'I know what a beauty case looks like. I'll find it.'

Lindsey closed her eyes. He'd told her to relax so she'd try. He'd taken over anyway. And right at the moment the idea sounded heaven-sent.

Dan was back. Not only did he have her beauty case but he'd brought along her shoulder bag as well. And her long woolly cardigan was draped over his forearm.

'You've thought of everything.' Lindsey managed a trapped smile.

'And I have something for your neck pain as well.'

'What are they?' She looked dubiously at the foil-wrapped tablets he handed her.

'They're standard painkillers,' Dan said. 'Nothing to send you off to la-la land.' He watched as she broke open the foil and then handed her a bottle of water. When she'd swallowed the tablets, he asked, 'Now, how are we going to do this?'

Lindsey blinked. He was obviously referring to her massage. She unzipped her beauty case and handed him the bottle of oil. 'I could probably just manoeuvre myself so my back's to you,' she said throatily.

'Or we could fold back the rear seat so you could lie down.'

'That's not necessary.' Lindsey was firm. 'Just take your jacket back, Dan, and I'll get my shirt off.'

Dan's eyes widened. His heart gave a sideways skip. 'OK...'

Lindsey undid the buttons and shrugged off the loose-fitting shirt to reveal a snug little vest top beneath. She sent him an innocent look. 'What?'

'Nothing.'

She managed a soft chuckle. 'Had you going there, didn't I, Daniel?'

'A guy can live in hope,' he countered, his mouth lifting at the corners. 'Now, give me that oil and we'll get started.'

Lindsey felt her body relax its tension as Dan's fingers began the gentle kneading of her neck muscles. It felt good, so good, and she wanted it to go on for ever...

Dan let his hands drift over the smooth column of her neck and then tease out the tense muscles at its base, almost hypnotised by the feel of her satin-smooth skin under his hands. 'It's Dante, by the way.'

'Really?' Lindsey's voice went high in disbelief.

'Really.'

'From the Italian poet of the Middle Ages?'

'At least you have the origin right,' he said. 'My sisters used to tell everyone I'd been named after a middle-aged poet.'

'Oh, poor you. Were you teased a lot?'

'Sometimes I felt like quietly enrolling at another school.'

'I think Dante suits you.'

'Hmm.' Dan was noncommittal.

'Is your mother a romantic, then?'

'No.' He sounded amused. 'It's an old family name. Apparently, it was just my turn to be lumbered with it.'

'That's pathetic,' Lindsey said mildly. 'It makes you different...*special*.'

He didn't reply.

'How does that feel now?'

Lindsey heard the guarded tone in his voice. Had her remark embarrassed him? Probably. And she wouldn't have continued with the banter if she hadn't been feeling so relaxed with him. Her mistake. 'It's much better, thanks. I'll be OK now.' She swivelled round to face the front again.

'If you're sure?' Dan recapped the bottle of oil and handed it back to her.

'I'm fine.' She stowed the bottle back in her beauty case then reached for her cardigan and shrugged it on.

Well, he'd stuffed that up. Dan locked his hands around the steering wheel and looked blindly out into the night. He'd stomped all over her light remarks and shut down. Now she'd be back to thinking he was some kind of unsociable cretin. God, he felt like an infant trying to stand upright and walk.

His jaw tightened. He had to fix things. 'I've…made things awkward again, haven't I?'

Her throat constricted. 'I wasn't coming on to you.'

'I know that. You were being sweet and funny…' He paused painfully.

'I've—been out of circulation for a while.'

Lindsey glanced at him, taking in his body language. Obviously, he'd been through something that had knocked him sideways. Something it was taking him time to get past. She felt a river of empathy run out to him. 'Do you want to talk about it?' As soon as she'd said the trite words Lindsey wished them back. Whatever it was that was bugging him, he'd probably *talked* about it until he was blue in the face. 'Sorry, scratch that.'

He blew out a controlled sigh. 'It's just stuff that's a bit hard to…revisit.'

'I get that, Dan,' she said softly.

His head swung towards her. Even in the subdued lighting in the car, the force of his undivided attention was like a mini-riot inside her. They breathed through several beats of silence. Until… Dan bent, his lips grazing hers. It was the lightest of kisses but heady with the taste of promise. For a long moment they stared at each other. 'That was a bit…' Lindsey's voice faded.

'Unexpected?' Dan moved closer, so close she had to tilt her head up to look at him. So close she could feel the heat radiating from his body. 'Nice, though?'

His softly spoken question danced across her nerves, creating a new wave of warmth to cascade through her. She nodded, words simply escaping her.

Dan stroked her cheek with the backs of his fingers, his body drenched in emotions he'd almost forgotten.

A gossamer-thin thread of awareness seemed to shimmer between them, until they drew back slowly from each other, breaking the spell.

Lindsey began pulling her cardigan more tightly around her. 'Um, do you think we could find a hot drink somewhere?'

'Oh, God—sorry!' Dan hit the heel of his hand on his forehead. 'You're probably still shocky. I'm an idiot—'

'Dan, it's OK.' Lindsey bit back a half-laugh. 'I didn't expect you to have a Thermos of tea with you. There's a service station a few clicks further on. We could stop there.'

'Right. Good. We'll do that. But we'll need to do something about your car first. From what I saw, it's not drivable.'

'Oh—are you sure?' Lindsey looked pained.

'I'm no mechanic but looks like you had a pretty big whack. The back wheel seems out of alignment and I had trouble getting the boot open. I could have a word with the tow-truck guys for you?'

'No, it's fine.' She waved the idea away. 'I'll get on to

my insurance company.' She flicked out her mobile and found the number on speed dial. 'All sorted,' she said after a few minutes of intense negotiation. 'They'll arrange for my car to be towed for repairs and if I need it I can pick up a replacement vehicle from the garage in Milldale.'

'I'll drive you home, then,' Dan said.

'I don't want to take you out of your way.'

'You won't be. I'm going to Milldale myself. I'll get your personal stuff from the car, shall I?'

'I'll help.' Lindsey volunteered, making to get out of his vehicle.

'Hang on a tick.' He stayed her with the lightest touch on her wrist. 'I'll come round and give you a hand. Don't want you falling.'

'Dan, I'm fine,' she remonstrated.

'Humour me, all right?'

Lindsey gave a contained little sigh but waited until he'd come round to the passenger door. He opened it and offered a steadying hand. She took it gratefully. He'd been right. She did feel a kind of light-headedness.

'When did you last eat?' Dan asked, keeping his hand firmly on hers.

'Sandwich at lunch.'

'Then the sooner we get some hot food into you the better.' He reopened the boot and retrieved her suitcase and a canvas backpack.

'And would you mind getting that large plastic bin as well?' Lindsey asked. 'It has a lid so you won't spill anything.'

Dan hefted the bin out by its handle, almost staggering at its solid weight. 'What the blazes do you have in here—body parts?'

Her mouth crimped at the corners. 'Clay.'

'I...see.' Although clearly he didn't.

'It's potter's clay,' Lindsey explained, following him

back to the Land Rover. 'I have a wheel and kiln at home. I aim to make some pieces while I'm on my holiday.'

Dan tried to get a grip on his wayward thoughts, imagining *Lindsey the potter* with her dark hair wild and flowing, perhaps her feet bare, her body lithe and swaying as she threw her pots. A compelling new awareness, sharp and insistent, stirred within him. An awareness that hadn't been stirred in a long time. An awareness that he'd stomped all over on that first day when Lindsey Stewart had smiled at him.

'Do you think you should let your folks know what's happened so they won't be worrying?' Dan asked as they settled back into the car. 'I imagine it'll be a bit late by the time we get you home.'

That sounded so thoughtful. Lindsey turned her head, slowly taking in his profile. It was almost sculpted. He'd make a perfect model. Her fingers began to tingle and she imagined carving out his features from a block of clay, pleating, smoothing, working her thumbs to form his cheekbones, a slow sweep to define his jaw, the touch of a finger defining the cleft in his chin. Definitely that. She pressed her thumb and forefinger together, almost feeling the slide of wet clay as she fashioned the curve of his mouth...

'Lindsey?'

'Uh—' She came back with a jolt.

'Do you need to ring home?'

'Actually, my parents are in Scotland, visiting my brother and sister-in-law. They've just had their first baby. Mum and Dad are away for a few more weeks yet.'

Dan started the engine and they began moving. 'So, who's at home for you, then?'

'I don't need looking after.'

'You've been through a trauma tonight, Lindsey. What if you need something—or someone?'

Heck! Was he offering? Lindsey pulled back from the flight of fancy. 'I should explain,' she said. 'We have managers for the vineyard, Jeff and Fiona Collins. Their cottage is quite close to the main house. Knowing I'm coming, Fi will have aired the place, stocked the fridge and left the lights on. I'll phone her when I arrive and she's around if I need anything.'

'I guess that's all right, then,' he said, as the bright lights of the roadhouse came into view.

'That was lovely, thanks.' Lindsey forked up the last of her omelette and then sat back, replete. 'So, why are you heading to Milldale?'

'Nathan Lyons's wedding.' Dan finished off his steak sandwich and casually swiped his mouth with the paper napkin.

'Of course. I can't believe I'd forgotten for the moment. It'll be a big do. Sami will have all the trimmings.'

Dan raised a dark brow. 'You know Sami?'

'For ever. Our parents' properties adjoin. We lost touch a bit when she relocated to Sydney but we've caught up again now she's back.'

'I'm Nathan's best man,' Dan said.

'I knew from the hospital grapevine you were mates.' Lindsey rested her chin in her upturned hand and looked at him. 'Are you looking forward to the wedding?'

'Yes, I am…' he said slowly, and realised it was true. 'They're a great couple.'

Lindsey gave a soft laugh. 'They're in love. It shows.'

'I suppose it does. Have *you* ever been in love, Lindsey?' he asked abruptly.

Wow! That was out of left field. 'In love. Out of love,' she sidestepped lightly. 'You?'

He gave a tight shrug. 'Same.'

They picked up their mugs of tea, each silently assessing the weight of their answers, each guessing that they hadn't exactly been lies but that they hadn't been quite the truth either.

'You're not Sami's bridesmaid, by any chance?' Dan asked after a minute.

'No. Her sister Caitlin's filling that role. She's just back from a modelling assignment overseas. Cait's the face of Avivia.'

'Which is…?'

Lindsey chuckled. 'Avivia is an international cosmetic company.'

'Ah.' He nodded sagely. 'But *you'll* be at the wedding?'

'Yes. I'll save you a dance,' she ventured daringly.

Dan's eyes flicked wide. The thought of dancing with her, *holding* her, sent a new chain of awareness shooting up his spine.

'I take it you *can* dance?'

'Yes, I can dance.' He gave a guarded kind of smile. 'In fact, I used to love dancing.'

'Used to?'

'It's been a while.'

'Oh.' Lindsey drew back in her chair. Out of nowhere, her body felt tingly with electricity. 'We'll have to catch you up, then.'

His chuckle was a bit rusty. 'Don't plan ahead too much. I think I'm supposed to dance with the bridesmaid a bit.'

'Well, only the first dance, perhaps.' Lindsey's eyes gleamed. She was enjoying this. 'Cait's engaged. She'll have her bloke with her.'

'So…' Dan considered. 'After the first dance, I'm off the hook?'

'Unless Nathan expects you to work the room.'

'Unlikely.' His mouth curved into a crooked moue that was almost a grin.

'That's good, then.' Suddenly Lindsey's breath felt fluttery. What was it about being with Dan that made her feel as though she was flying through space without a parachute?

And loving it?

CHAPTER FOUR

THE NEXT MORNING Dan was awake early. He got up, embracing a new sense of purpose, a kind of upbeat feeling, as he threw himself into the shower and then dressed in faded jeans and a long-sleeved navy T-shirt. He'd arranged to meet Nathan for breakfast.

He slipped quietly down the stairs from the upper floor of the pub and stepped out onto the street. So this was Milldale, Lindsey's family home. He could imagine her growing up here, he thought. A leggy country kid, bright as newly minted gold, a bit sassy, self-reliant... He shook the image away and continued along the quaint village street.

He checked his watch. He had time to spare for a walk and gain his bearings. Hope for something he couldn't quite define was springing up in his heart as he continued on his walk. The main street gave way to a few houses, a park and an unexpectedly steep hill. Full of energy, Dan climbed the hill to a viewing platform that overlooked the surrounding countryside. He leaned on the safety rail and looked out. The view seemed never-ending, timeless, stretching from the early spring greenness of the vineyards to the gentle rise and fall of blue hills beyond. Houses were dotted through the vineyards, a wisp of smoke drifting from one of the chimneys.

He took a cleansing breath so deep it almost hurt. Today was the first day of the rest of his life. He couldn't wait to see what it might bring.

'You're almost a married man,' Dan addressed Nathan as they sat over their traditional English breakfast.

'Can't wait.' Nathan added a curl of bacon to his egg. 'I'm sorry it didn't work out for you, mate,' he said quietly.

Dan gave a rough laugh. 'Well, the circumstances were hardly ideal, were they? Not like you and Sami. Even Lindsey remarked how "in love" the pair of you seem.'

'You mean it shows?' Nathan's face was lit with a goofy grin.

'Just a bit. Make sure it stays that way,' Dan said.

'Oh, man.' Nathan lifted his gaze briefly to the ceiling. 'You're not about to give me a *talk*, are you?'

'No. But I need to say something before we get caught up in all the hoopla. I can't count the number of times you've had my back, Nathan. You've been the best mate. The best. I hope you and Sami have the most amazing life together.'

'Thanks,' Nathan responded, a bit gruffly. 'That means a lot, Dan. But friendship is a two-way street. I'd like to think we've both had each other's backs over the years. Right, I could go another round of toast.' He broke what could have been an awkward male moment and hailed a passing waitress. 'Speaking of Lindsey...' he gave Dan an enquiring look '...how is she after last night's MVA? Have you called her?'

'It's a bit early yet.'

'And the injured guy?' Nathan asked.

'Induced coma. That's all they're prepared to say.' Dan placed his knife and fork neatly together on his plate. 'Uh—did you know Lindsey's into pottery?'

'Yeah. Lins is a seriously talented artist. When the

new maternity wing opened last year she gifted a mother-and-child sculpture for the foyer. You should take a ride to the fourth floor and poke your head in some time.'

'Maybe I'll do that,' Dan said, knowing he wouldn't. But that was his business. He poured a second cup of tea and gave himself permission to relax, to shuck off the negative thoughts Nathan's suggestion had set running.

Today was about new beginnings.

The wedding was wonderful, the best man's speech a triumph. Dan's remarks were warm and lively, with just the right amount of wit, nicely balanced with sincerity and in keeping with the significance of the occasion.

Lindsey joined in the applause as Dan resumed his seat. For some reason she couldn't define, she felt inordinately proud of him.

The remainder of the speeches were heartfelt but brief and the newlyweds took to the floor for the first dance. Almost as if her eyes were hotwired in Dan's direction, Lindsey saw him incline his head towards Caitlin. Caitlin smiled and they rose together. Obviously, they were about to join Nathan and Sami on the dance floor. Lindsey made a dry little swallow. Dan seemed very much at ease as he whirled Caitlin into an old-fashioned waltz. They looked stunning together. And Lindsey was swamped with jealousy. Taking up her glass, she took a gulp of her champagne and pretended not to care.

'Dance, Lindsey?'

Lindsey brought her head up sharply to find Eliot Swift, one of Sami's cousins, hovering. He'd come to Milldale for holidays when they'd all been in their teens. He'd had a bit of a crush on her then. Her eyes widened. 'Hi, Eliot. I didn't know you were here.'

He grimaced. 'Big crowd. You on your own?'

She nodded. Well, she *was*, wasn't she? Eliot held out

his hand and she took it and let him guide her across to
the dance floor.

'Been a while.' He sent her a wry smile.

'Yes. What have you been up to?'

'Selling IT to the masses. Travelling a bit. You?'

'Travelling a bit as well. Presently nursing at Hopeton
District.'

'Ah.' His eyes held a glimmer of humour. 'Found your
niche, then.'

'I believe so.'

'Great summers back then, weren't they?'

'Mmm. But now we've all grown up. Are you married?'

'Nah.' He shook his head, and they took to the floor.
'Sorry, was that your foot?'

'One of them.' Lindsey laughed. She couldn't help herself. They could have been seventeen again and she could
have been back on the Kellys' veranda, trying to teach
Eliot to dance.

'I still can't waltz,' he apologised. 'But we can shuf-
fle about until they change the tempo. Shouldn't be long.
Ah, good.' He sounded relieved as the music changed into
something slow and torchy and he gathered her in with
style.

Dan frowned a bit, catching sight of Lindsey as she
danced past. She was wearing a red dress, one smooth
shoulder exposed, her hair loose and shiny. She looked…
beautiful. Dan's interest intensified as he checked out her
partner. They looked pretty cosy. And he was holding
Lindsey far too close. Dan felt his gut curl into an uncomfortable knot. *He* was the one who should have been
holding her.

For the next while Lindsey danced and mingled. She
stopped to chat with Sami's mother, Marcia, and assured
her it was a marvellous wedding. And, yes, she, Lindsey,
was having a fine time.

'Oh—excuse me, love.' Marcia turned in response to some urgent hand gesturing from one of the catering people and took off.

Lindsey took a relieved breath. This was her cue to slip outside for some air.

It was a cool evening, and because much of the gracious old home's beauty lay in its outdoors, the verandas were spectacularly lit, fairy-lights peeped out of boxed hedges arranged beside the door, and glossy-leaved potted plants were decorated with love hearts and sparkly bows. Lindsey's mouth tipped into a wry smile. It seemed Sami had indeed got her trimmings.

Descending the shallow flight of stairs to the sweeping lawn beyond, she looked up and gave a little breath of delight. The fairy-lights sprinkled around in the trees gave a storybook feel. It was the perfect setting for a wedding, she decided, sitting down on one of the old-fashioned garden benches.

She rested her head back on the wooden slats, looking up to the clear sky and the twinkling necklace of stars.

The light strains of the music floated out on the night air. After a while she heard the change to the thump, thump of an upbeat rhythm. Was Dan still dancing with Caitlin? She'd heard a discreet whisper that Caitlin's engagement was off. Perhaps Dan would feel obliged to partner her for most of the evening. But from what she'd seen, it hadn't seemed much of a hardship for him. She shivered slightly. Obviously, he'd forgotten about *their* dance.

She closed her eyes.

'Hey…'

Lindsey's eyes snapped open. 'Dan!' She swallowed jerkily.

He sat beside her. 'I've been looking for you everywhere. I meant to call you but I got caught up. It's been like a circus all day and then the wedding…'

'Well, you had to expect that.' Lindsey gave a little shrug. 'You are the best man.'

'Last night was pretty rough.' Dan paused and looked at her. 'Did you manage to sleep all right?'

'Yes.' Lindsey turned her face up to his. Even in the half-light she could see the concern in his eyes. It unsettled her to realise how relieved she felt. She hadn't imagined the closeness of last night. It seemed he did care. 'In fact, I slept in. And Fiona's been like a mother hen all day.' She sent him a guarded smile. 'I'm fine.'

'You look amazing.' He lowered his head slightly, so close his chin was almost dusting her cheek.

Her breath caught on a stilted laugh. 'So do you.'

'I take it, then, we're both pretty amazing.' His eyes gleamed with intent.

Her stomach curled. He'd taken off his suit jacket, loosened his tie and rolled his sleeves back over his forearms. She took a breath, the subtle scent of his aftershave filling her nostrils. 'I thought you'd forgotten our dance.'

'Was that likely?' His mouth went to where her neck met her shoulder in the softest caress.

Lindsey's eyes drifted shut and she shivered.

'I had to have a couple of duty dances,' Dan said, 'with Nathan's mum and his Aunt Tilly.'

'The large lady in the purple pants suit? She looked formidable.'

'But a great dancer,' Dan proclaimed, his lips twitching. 'She runs a pub in Sydney.' His gaze went to Lindsey's mouth and lingered. 'Why are we having this crazy conversation? When we should be doing this…'

Lindsey swallowed, her heart banging out of rhythm. Racing. He was bending towards her, his blue eyes capturing hers with a magnetic pull. 'Dan…?'

'Don't talk…' In an almost imperceptible movement he slid his hands beneath her elbows and they rose as one.

Instantly, Lindsey felt her nerve ends tingling, her breathing uncomfortably tight. She lifted her head, searing her gaze with his.

'I need to do this again…' Dan reached up, sliding the tips of his fingers over her face, feeling the gentle throb of heat under her skin, the feminine, fragile line of her jaw. Even as his thumb lifted her chin his fingers were seeking her nape, drawing her to him.

He lowered his head slowly, giving her the chance to end it, if that's what she wanted. But she didn't, and her lips gave a tiny sigh of welcome as his mouth brushed hers, settling over its softness with touch-and-retreat little sips, feeling the instant response and teasing her lips into a more open kiss.

Lindsey was drowning in feelings she hadn't experienced for the longest time. Dan's mouth on hers felt right, their kiss pure and perfect. So dazzlingly perfect. He drew her closer and she opened her mouth as though to savour and hold onto the magic of his kiss, walking her fingers to the curve of his neck and into the soft strands of his hair.

And she didn't let herself think for one second whether any of what they were sharing had a future. She was just amazed that they should be kissing at all and that she'd so longed for it without even knowing why…

'You have the sweetest mouth,' Dan murmured much later, moving his hands to her shoulders and then cupping her face in his hands.

She licked her lips. 'Do I?'

'Mmm.' He bent to her again, pressing his forehead to hers. It seemed a lifetime later when Dan drew back. He took her hands, absently running his thumbs across her knuckles. 'I suppose we should get back in there.'

'Yes, I suppose we should.' Lindsey reluctantly withdrew her hands, swiping a fall of hair back over her shoulder. 'I imagine the bride and groom will want to get away soon.'

'Come on, then.' Dan held out his hand and they were linked again. As they made their way back indoors to Rosemount's beautiful ballroom, they saw the crowd gathering for the farewells. 'I'd better have a word with Nate,' Dan said. 'He looks like a rogue bull caught in the headlights.'

Nathan's relief when he saw Dan was almost palpable. 'Sami and I want to split. Any ideas for a quick getaway?'

'I'll alert the limo driver.' Dan pulled out his mobile, his eyes assessing a possible exit route. 'Have you said your private farewells?'

'All done. And, mate…' Nathan slung his arm around Dan's shoulders. 'Thanks. And I mean for the classic speech and, well, for everything.'

'It's been a great day.' Dan's jaw worked a bit. 'You and Sami have a fantastic honeymoon. Where is she, by the way?'

'Just here.' Sami materialised beside them and linked her arm through Nathan's. 'Are we heading off, babe?' She turned a very sweet smile on her new husband.

'As soon as Dan can find us an escape route.' Nathan bent and pressed a kiss into his wife's hair.

'Dan.' Sami let go of Nathan's arm and turned to Dan, kissing him on both cheeks. 'Thank you so much. You've been the best best man! Oops!' She put a finger to her smiling mouth. 'I think I've had a bit much champagne. But you know what I mean.'

'It's been fun, Sami,' Dan said. 'Take care of this big guy.'

'Take care of each other,' Lindsey chimed in, and hugged them both.

'Oh, Lins.' Sami whisked Lindsey aside. 'Keep an eye

on Cait, would you? She's a bit emotional about…well, you know…'

Lindsey nodded. 'Don't worry, Eliot's taken Cait under his wing.'

'Good old El.' Sami sent Lindsey an arch look. 'He still has a thing for you, you know?'

Lindsey just grinned. 'In your dreams, Samantha. Oh, look, Dan's beckoning. Grab Nathan and scoot.'

'Thanks for everything, guys!' Sami threw back over her shoulder as Nathan took her hand and urged her swiftly through the blaze of farewells and good wishes to the white stretch limousine in the forecourt.

Lindsey smiled softly as they watched the car drive out of sight. 'Wasn't it the loveliest wedding?'

'Yes, it was…' Dan's thoughts winged back to another time, another wedding…

'You OK?' Lindsey asked, realising he'd gone quiet.

Dan blew out a breath that untied the sudden knots in his stomach. 'Bit nostalgic,' he admitted, and threaded his fingers through hers.

'You and Nathan go back a long way, don't you?'

'First day at uni. Shared a house through our training…'

'Parties and girls,' Lindsey surmised, and smiled at him.

He gave a half-shrug. 'All that. I'm immensely happy for him.'

'So, you believe in marriage, then?' she said casually, although her antenna was tuned for his answer.

His look became shuttered. 'Well, people seem to be still doing it.'

And that, decided Lindsey, was no answer at all.

They headed back inside. 'My duties as best man are all done,' Dan said. 'The band is on a break, so perhaps we could find somewhere less noisy and have a drink? I believe the champagne is still flowing.'

Lindsey made a small face. 'I think I'd actually prefer some tea.'

* * *

They made their way through to a kind of garden room where a helpful waiter organised their pot of tea. Lindsey poured, saying, 'I'm assuming you have the rest of the weekend off?'

'Actually, I have a few days' leave.' Dan took the cup she handed across to him. 'I pulled some extra shifts to make it happen.'

'Oh.' The tip of Lindsey's tongue roved her bottom lip. So that was the reason she'd kept missing him at work. He'd been off when she'd been on. 'You must be running on empty, then, with the wedding on top of everything.'

He shrugged. 'I'll recharge quickly.'

Lindsey's heartbeat picked up a notch and an idea began forming. 'So…what are you doing with your time off?'

'I haven't quite decided yet. I have the use of an apartment at the Gold Coast whenever I want it. Maybe I could catch some waves. A bit of sun. A bit of fun.'

Fun? Lindsey dropped her gaze. Did that mean a holiday fling while he was at the coast? That idea didn't gel at all. She tilted her head back to look at him properly. 'Do you have friends at the coast?'

'No.' Dan's eyes seemed to track over her features one by one before he went on. 'I'm used to being on my own. It doesn't bother me.'

Well, it should. Lindsey's fingers spanned her teacup. Was Dan Rossi a loner by choice? She didn't think so. She'd seen how much he'd enjoyed the social interaction at the wedding. And he hadn't been faking it. He'd been warm and funny. And sexy…

However hard she tried, she couldn't remain detached. That assumption had been shattered like eggshells under a heavy boot the moment they'd tasted each other. She'd loved the way he'd kissed. So many men didn't know how to kiss, she thought. But Dan had it down in spades. Or maybe it was simply that their bodies were totally in tune, their chemistry perfect for each other. She felt her skin prickle at the thought. Suddenly she straightened in her chair. Like a spark on tinder, the idea turned into possibility. 'I have a much better idea. You could spend your days off here in Milldale. With me.'

Dan looked up, startled. 'With you,' he repeated.

'Well, not exactly *with me*,' Lindsey explained. 'What I meant to say was that we have several holiday cabins at the vineyard. You could have one of those—if you wanted to, of course.'

'Uh-huh.'

Oh, God, she thought as her heart began pattering. She couldn't believe what she'd just done. It was so unlike her. She'd jumped in boots and all and had probably put Dan on the spot. But he was a grown-up, she justified. He could say no. 'There are hiking trails if that appeals, heated pool and spa up at the house. Soft blue sky days and the quiet just seem to settle around you. There's no feeling quite like it. It kind of all ties together; the peace and the feeling you can let go and just...*be*.'

Be. Dan's breath jammed in his throat. One tiny word with a thousand connotations. Her eyes had turned almost silver. Here I am, they seemed to say. So why on earth was he hesitating? Unless his instincts were leading him astray, Lindsey Stewart was the real deal. Lovely, exciting. Sexy. He felt a wild heat in every part of his body.

And he hadn't had a feeling like this about a woman for the longest time.

Somehow their hands had met across the table, their fingertips touching.

'That sounds excellent,' he said almost formally. 'I'll be happy to accept your invitation, Lindsey.'

Lindsey watched as his mouth quirked with humour and acknowledged the almost painful lurching of her heart as it thundered out the heated rhythm of physical attraction. 'Oh, ha-ha.' She took her hand away, realising she'd worried about nothing. 'You're taking the mickey, aren't you?'

His grin unfolded lazily, his eyes crinkling at the corners. 'You looked so earnest selling me your idea, Lindsey, when in reality you didn't have to sell it to me at all.' Reaching across, he took her hand again, slowly interlinking his fingers through hers. A tiny pulse flickered in his cheek. 'I'd love to spend my days off with you.' He fiddled with the gold filigree ring she wore on her middle finger. 'Perhaps we could just *be* together?'

Her eyes slanted, their expression sultry and soft. 'Perhaps we could.' She reclaimed her hand gently. 'Now I'm going to call it a night.' Picking up her clutch bag, she held it against her chest. 'You know the way to Lark Hill so I'll see you tomorrow, shall I?'

Dan was immediately alert. 'How are you getting home?'

'Cab. I imagine all of Milldale's taxi fleet is on duty tonight.'

'My car's here. I'll drive you.'

'Dan.' Lindsey shook her head. 'It's not necessary. You've had a long day—'

She watched his mouth firm.

'I'll drive you home.'

CHAPTER FIVE

LINDSEY WOKE WITH a start on Sunday morning. She grabbed her phone off the bedside table and fell back against her pillow. It was just eight o'clock. Dan probably wouldn't be here for ages yet.

A smile touched her mouth and widened to a full-blown grin. The good Dr Rossi thought he'd played the cool card but she knew her invitation had rattled his composure. She was still a little amazed that she'd asked him to spend his leave with her. But the invitation had bubbled out from somewhere deep within her.

And just maybe it was all meant to be.

When her phone rang she was still hugging the thought. Checking the caller ID, she felt a thrilling reality. 'Dan, hi.'

'Ms Stewart, I presume. Are you up?'

'Of course.' She hastily levered herself upright and swung to the side of the bed. 'Are you?'

'Yes.' He didn't tell her he'd already been to Hopeton and back to collect some extra clothes for his impromptu holiday.

'Are you still at the pub?'

'Actually, no,' he said easily. 'I'm only a few minutes away from you.'

'You are!' Lindsey almost squeaked. Abruptly, she ended the call and sprinted to the bathroom.

What to wear? Back in her bedroom, she shuffled

through the clothes she still hadn't unpacked from her suitcase. She took out her soft jeans, a white T-shirt and, because she felt a lingering chill of winter in the air, she shrugged into a little cropped-style cardigan. Now shoes—

As the sound of the old-fashioned door knocker echoed along the hallway, she spun to a halt. He was here! And she felt only half-dressed. Hastily, she shoved her feet into ballet flats, finger-combed her hair and went to let him in.

'Dan…' She blinked out into the early-morning sunlight and felt a soft shiver like a slipstream of desire feather all the way down her backbone. He looked so early-morning sexy with the beginnings of a dark shadow along his jaw and the simple male thing of the collar of his check shirt all askew under his navy jumper. She made a little sound in her throat.

Just the sight of her curled a wild kind of excitement through Dan's gut. She had no make-up on. No lingering smell of perfume. But she exuded a kind of femaleness that was…intoxicating. A bubble of pure want exploded inside him. He took a step forward.

In a second they were leaning into each other.

Dan's mouth moved against hers, shaping her name as their bodies aligned. And then he kissed her, a gentle, sweet, slow kiss that tingled all the way down to her toes, before he let her go. 'Good morning,' she said softly.

He lifted a strand of her hair and wound it around his finger. '*Now* it is,' he said.

She gave him one of her wide smiles, activating the dimples beside her mouth. 'Come through. Have you eaten?'

'I had a coffee earlier.'

'Let's see what the pantry can yield up, then,' she said, leading the way along the hallway to the kitchen.

Dan took a quick inventory of the timber benches and

the navy blue and white tiles. 'Big workspaces,' he commented. 'Do you cater for your guests as well?'

'The cabins allow for self-catering,' Lindsey said, 'but sometimes we provide breakfast baskets if anyone requests them. I'll fix something for us now. What would you like?'

'Anything is fine. Surprise me.'

She flipped him a cheeky grin. 'I think I have already.'

She had. And his mind still couldn't quite grasp the fact that he was here with her. In her home. About to share breakfast with her. His gaze jagged across her face. 'I can't believe I'm actually here.'

'Of course you're here.' Her lashes swooped, eyeing him from head to toe. 'Otherwise who have I just kissed?'

Dan gave a gravelly laugh and looked around the room, his gaze lighting on the sun-catcher crystal that dangled from the window in front of the sink. 'Nice *feng shui*.'

Lindsey raised an eyebrow at the abrupt change in conversation. 'You a follower, then?'

He shrugged. 'Parts of the philosophy appeal to me.'

Who'd have thought? Now he'd surprised *her*. Lindsey loaded crockery and cutlery onto a tray and set them on the bench.

'What can I do to help?' Dan asked.

'Let's eat outside on the back deck,' she said, handing him the tray. 'Could you set the table?'

'I think I can manage that.'

Male distraction gone for the moment, Lindsey set about preparing breakfast. She juiced oranges and deftly arranged portions of melon and a variety of other fruit on a glass platter. That would do for starters, she decided, picking up the plate.

Dan was leaning over the railing, looking into the distance. He turned to Lindsey as she came to stand beside him. 'This is God's own country,' he said, a faraway look in his eyes. 'How can you bear to leave it and go to work in a casualty department?'

She sent him a pained look. 'Now you're talking like a tourist. Running a successful vineyard is extremely hard work, Dan. You can't sit around, admiring the scenery.'

His mouth quirked. 'And that's what you do in Casualty?'

She made a face at him. 'That's the creek down there.' She pointed out an unbroken line of willows. 'Sami, Cait, my brother James and I had some fun times there when we were growing up.'

'I can imagine.' Dan sent her a soft look. 'James is your brother who's in Scotland, right?'

'Yes. He and his wife, Catherine, are physiotherapists. Their baby daughter, Alexandra Rose, is just three weeks old.'

'Nice name.' Dan felt an uncomfortable tightening in his gut and breathed it away. 'And the cabins?'

'There are four. See, over there to your left.' She indicated the weathered timber structures nestled into the side of the hill. 'You can get settled in later.' She touched his forearm. 'Shall we eat, then?'

'So, how come the name Lark Hill?' Dan asked, as they each took a selection of fruit. 'As far as I know, we have no larks as such in Australia.'

'Long story short,' Lindsey said, popping a sliver of golden kiwi fruit into her mouth, 'my great-grandparents came from England. When they came to Milldale to begin farming, the bird calls reminded them of the larks back home. But of course they were our magpie larks, better known as peewees. But they'd already registered the place as Lark Hill so it just stayed.'

'Fascinating,' Dan said. 'So your family are literally pioneers of the district.'

Lindsey lifted a shoulder. 'It just feels like we've always been here, I suppose. What about the Rossi family, then?'

Dan's mouth puckered briefly. 'I don't think we're pioneers of anything—except maybe passing down old names.'

Lindsey *tsked*. 'I really meant whereabouts are you from?'

'Melbourne.'

'You mentioned sisters. Any more siblings?'

Dan shook his head. 'I suppose you want a rundown.' He gave a resigned lopsided grin.

'Of course. Then I'll know where to put you in your family.'

Dan lifted an eyebrow and helped himself to a sliver of melon. 'My dad is a linguistics professor at Melbourne Uni. Mum is a director of early childhood education.'

'Wow.' Lindsey lifted a hand, casually swinging her index finger through a long curl as it fell against her throat. 'I'll bet some interesting conversations happened there.'

'Mmm.' Dan sucked the sweet juice of the melon deeply into his mouth. 'They're both pretty passionate about learning. I think the girls and I could read before we could walk,' he joked.

'And your sisters,' Lindsey asked interestedly. 'Younger? Older?'

'Younger.'

'And what are they—lawyers, doctors?'

'No.' He gave an amused chuckle. 'Juliana trained as a teacher-librarian but now she runs a combined bookshop and coffee corner in downtown Melbourne. Reg—Regina—is married to Christoph. They're both professional musicians, violinists with the Melbourne Symphony Orchestra.'

Lindsey drank the information in. 'So, you're rather an arts-related kind of family, then. Rich in good conversation, music, books and so on.'

'I suppose.'

So, in fact, quite similar to her own background, Lindsey thought. 'But you obviously broke the mould and opted for the sciences and medicine. How did that happen?'

'My uncle Robert, Dad's brother, is a physician,' Dan explained. 'He arrived late in their family so to us kids he was more like a big brother than an uncle. I hung out with Rob a bit. And with his skeleton,' he added with a smile. 'I was always fascinated with the idea of becoming a doctor.'

'You weren't daunted by the study involved?'

He shook his head. 'Couldn't get enough of it.'

'It's a real calling for you, then.'

'Becoming a doctor? I guess it was.' Dan chased the last piece of fruit around his bowl and thought with something like amazement that it had been an age since he'd talked so freely about himself. But then again Lindsey seemed to have that effect on him. There was an openness about her that called to him to respond in a similar way. He leaned back in his chair, eyeing her thoughtfully.

'What?' Lindsey flicked him a startled look. His gaze had gone all smoky.

'Just thinking. This is good, isn't it?'

'This?' Her eyes widened and lit.

'This. Us. Here.'

Lindsey tipped her head on one side and looked searchingly at him. His voice had held slight wonder. 'Yes, it is,' she said, and thought that on a personal level they probably still had a few mountains to climb. But what was a mountain or two when Lark Hill was beginning to work its magic already...

'Well, come on, Ms Stewart.' Dan broke into her thoughts. 'That's me done. What about you and nursing?'

Lindsey batted the question away. 'There's not all that much to tell. I actually thought seriously about medicine but I'm a hands-on kind of girl. I figured it would be ages before I could do anything useful as a doctor, whereas nursing offered the chance to get stuck in fairly quickly,' she summed up with a smile. 'And here I am.'

Dan's gaze softened. 'Indeed you are.'

Deflecting his scrutiny, Lindsey hurriedly got to her feet and began collecting their used dishes. 'Shall we make some toast? Fiona's left one of her special wattle-seed loaves.'

'Sounds interesting.' Dan pushed himself upright and took the tray from her and they made their way back to the kitchen.

An hour later they were on their second pot of tea and still talking. About anything and everything. And it had all seemed as natural as breathing, Lindsey thought. In fact, so engrossed had they become, neither heard the sound of the front door opening and closing or the soft footfall along the hallway until, 'Yoo-hoo. It's only me. Are you there, Lindsey?'

'It's Fiona.' Lindsey put a finger to her lips. 'Be prepared to be well looked over. On the deck, Fi,' she called.

Fiona, cropped greying hair and with the suntanned complexion of her outdoor lifestyle, came out onto the deck and stopped, her clear blue gaze running assessingly over them. 'Not interrupting, am I?'

'Of course you're not.' Lindsey sought to put the older woman at ease. 'This is Dan Rossi. He's a friend from the hospital.'

Dan rose courteously and they shook hands. 'Nice to meet you, Fiona.'

'And you, Dan.' Fiona's gaze widened as something clicked. 'You're the doctor who kindly brought this one home after the accident, then?'

'That's me.' He shot a slightly mocking look at Lindsey. 'I think she'd have tried to walk home if I'd let her.'

Fiona shook her head. 'Independent to a fault. Always has been.'

'Hey, you two,' Lindsey protested. 'Do you mind?' She beckoned Fiona to a chair. 'Tea's still fresh.'

'No, thanks, love.' Fiona sat. 'I really just popped in to tell you I've let the last cabin.'

'Oh—OK… Who are the new people?'

'Young couple, Scott and Amy Fraser. Having a few days' holiday before the birth of their first baby.'

'A babymoon.' Lindsey smiled. 'That's so sweet.'

'They arrived last night,' Fiona said. 'Just saw them a while ago. They're off picnicking.'

'Well, it's a beautiful day so let's hope they enjoy the peace and quiet.' Lindsey looked at Dan. 'We should get out and stretch our legs too.'

With Fiona gone, they went inside, washed up and put the kitchen back to rights. Dan shoved the last of the cutlery into the drawer. 'I'll go back and stay at the pub tonight.'

'Why would you do that?' Lindsey hung the damp tea towel near the AGA to dry.

'Fiona said she's let the last cabin.'

'Stay here, then,' Lindsey countered practically. 'There's a guest bedroom you can have. It has its own en suite so you can be as private as you want to be.'

'Ah…' Dan swiped a hand across his cheekbones.

Watching his body language, Lindsey gave a little huff of disbelief. 'Surely you're not obsessing about propriety?'

He frowned through a beat.

'That's so sweetly old-fashioned.' Leaning back against the benchtop, she let her eyes rest softly on him. 'You're so well brought up, aren't you?'

Dan snorted. 'Give me a break. It's a small community. You and your family obviously have a certain…status.' And he hadn't missed Fiona's overt curiosity in his presence.

'Dan...'

'What?'

She stepped closer to him, her green eyes almost translucent as she met his gaze. 'We're grown-ups, aren't we?'

'I'd say so,' he murmured gruffly. 'Very grown-up...' he added, as he wound her hair loosely around his fingers, using the impetus to draw her closer and find her mouth.

They kissed long and hard until Dan let her go with a last lingering touch to her lips. 'Ah, Lindsey...' His fingers lifted her chin, his mouth only a breath away as he said her name again. 'Lindsey...'

'That's me.' She reached out to stroke his face, feeling his skin faintly, deliciously rough.

'I'll stay here then.'

Watching his mouth, so sexy in repose, Lindsey felt her heart pick up speed. 'I'm glad you've decided that. Now I won't have to put my fallback plan into action.'

He raised a brow in query.

'I was going to wrestle you for your car keys.'

'What's with you Milldale women?' Dan shook his head. 'Nathan said Sami was prone to wrestling *him*.'

'Must be something in the wine we grow,' Lindsey challenged, laughing, as Dan spun her away, as if they were about to dance. She shimmied back to him and locked her arms around his waist.

Dan's gaze heated. 'Now what...?'

She lifted her hand and traced the outline of his lips with her finger, recognising there was a new awareness beating its wings all around them. 'A walk perhaps?'

Or seventeen cold showers, Dan thought darkly, his mouth achingly sensitised by her touch.

Or he could give in to the avalanche of emotions engulfing him. And take her to bed.

Suddenly, making love with Lindsey seemed a natural progression from where they were now. The last step in intimacy. But perhaps he was fantasising. It had been so long since he'd been this close to a woman.

Had wanted to be this close.

So…all things considered, a walk, preferably a long one, would probably be a better option.

'Go get your stuff from the car,' Lindsey said, her gaze alight. 'I'll sort out some bed linen.'

CHAPTER SIX

'THIS IS GOING to be magic,' Lindsey said, as they walked through the vines, and then she showed Dan the creek and the rock pool. 'Next time you come, we'll swim here,' she said.

'So, I'm coming again…?' Dan held her loosely, looking deeply into her eyes.

He'd spoken quietly, his voice so husky it had made Lindsey shiver. 'Of course you are.' Wrapping her arms round his neck, she stepped closer to him so that they were hard against each other. And they kissed.

'So…' he said, when they'd broken apart.

'So…' she echoed.

'Funny how things turn out.'

'Mmm.'

They linked hands and continued on their hike. 'Should we be on the lookout for snakes?' Dan queried.

'Only elephants,' she deadpanned.

'I see.' Dan did a little sidestep away from her then pulled her back in. 'I've taken up with a joker.'

Further on, she challenged him to walk across the old bush log that spanned the deepest part of the creek. Dan obliged, easily and gracefully, arms held out like a tightrope walker to keep his balance. He gave a bow when he reached the other side and she made a face at him, before stepping lightly across the length of the log and joining him on the other side.

'Now where?' Dan asked as he gathered her in and spun her round.

'Up there.' Lindsey pointed to the highest point of the paddock. 'It looks steep but it's really a steady climb and then you get a great view.'

'And survey your domain,' he teased as they wandered off again.

'This is as far as we go,' Lindsey said when they reached the top of the hill.

Dan stopped and wheeled her round, linking his arms around her from behind. 'Ah...*bella vista*.'

'Pretty special, isn't it?' Eyes half-closed, Lindsey placed her hands on his forearms, almost absently stroking her fingers over his skin. She tipped her head back to look at him. 'Makes you feel good to be alive, doesn't it?'

'That—and being with you,' Dan added, a throaty edge to his voice.

They sat in a patch of dappled shade beneath a leopard tree, easing back against the trunk, their shoulders touching. For a long time they did little else other than absorb the gentle landscape and breathe in the air that was heady with the scent of wattles that edged up the hill and along the walking tracks.

'So, why New York, Dan?' His head jerked up as if she'd activated a string and she added quickly, 'Am I being too nosy?'

'No...' He pulled off a blade of grass and began shredding it with his fingers. 'I'd been there a couple of times on holidays, loved the buzz. When the chance came to work there, I grabbed it. The rest, as they say, is history. What about you?' He changed conversational lanes deftly. 'Travelled much?'

'Quite a bit.' Lindsey smiled up at him. 'The UK, of

course, seeing that James and Catherine live in Scotland. That was brilliant. We did some of Europe together. And last year I went to Japan for the snowboarding.'

'You're a snowboarder?' There was admiration in Dan's voice.

'Did you travel with a group?'

She shook her head. 'It probably would have been better if I had. I went with my boyfriend at the time.' She pulled her knees up to her chin and looked out into the distance. 'The day after we arrived he hooked up with one of the tour guides.'

'Ouch.'

Lindsey rolled her eyes in disdain. 'He described her as *cute* and said it was just a holiday fling. That it needn't change anything between us. The awful part was that it was all going on under my nose. How dumb was I?'

'I wouldn't call it dumb,' Dan said quietly. 'You trusted him and he let you down.' He brushed his fingers down her cheek. 'His loss, I think.' A long beat of silence until, 'I got married in New York.'

Married. The word fell like the thud of a stone into a deep pool. Lindsey's stomach began turning cartwheels. If he'd been going for shock value, he'd got it. She hesitated before asking, 'Are you still—?'

'No.' The word was snapped out. And then more or less on a sigh, 'We crashed and burned.'

Lindsey raised her gaze to look at him. That sounded awful. But he couldn't drop a major detail like that into the conversation and expect her to leave it there without comment. 'Do you want to tell me about it?'

Dan eased his back against the trunk of the tree, unaware his eyes had assumed a bleak look. He clamped his jaw and agonised over whether now was the time to tell Lindsey everything, but his gut did a somersault at the thought of resurrecting it all. He rubbed a hand across his cheekbones, feeling the familiar tightening in his throat, but he realised that if there was any chance of deepening his relationship with Lindsey, he had to plough on. 'Caroline and I met at a party. She was from out of state, an attorney, new to the city as I was. We began dating, doing stuff together...'

'OK. Fast forward all that. Obviously, you fell in love and got married.'

Dan averted his eyes quickly but not before she saw the pain in them.

She held out her hand to him. 'Sorry...that was glib.'

He took the hand she offered, pressing her fingers tightly as if to gain strength from the contact, then let it go. 'I imagine you've heard of the expression about your life turning on a dime?'

'Is—is that what happened to yours?'

'More or less.' There was silence as if he was searching for the words and then he began to talk very quietly and measuredly. 'When we met, we were both in crummy apartments so it seemed reasonable to move into something better and share the rent.'

'As a couple?'

'Well, it didn't start out like that and it wasn't something we'd planned.'

Lindsey frowned a bit. That didn't sound like the love affair of the century so why had they got married? Unless...?

'Caroline got pregnant.' His voice flattened. 'Down to a glitch in her contraception. She was panic-stricken. Her parents were...protective, ultra-conservative in their outlook, so totally proud of their only child when she'd got a place at one of the city's prestigious law firms, convinced she'd make partner in a few years. She was fearful of telling them about the pregnancy, distressed she'd let them down in some way. She said if she could tell them we were getting married, it would lessen the shock.'

Lindsey could hear the thudding of her own heart. She paused and frowned. 'And you married her?'

Dan registered her look of disbelief. 'It was my child too, Lindsey,' he justified. 'And I thought…well, if we put our best into the relationship, we could make it work. Then life began throwing us curveballs. We found out Caroline was carrying twins and that was scary enough but then we discovered they were mono-mono.'

Lindsey's breathing faltered. She interpreted what he was saying, that the babies had shared the same amniotic sac and the same placenta within the mother's uterus. 'That's extremely rare, isn't it?'

'Only in one per cent of pregnancies.' Dan looked out into the distance. 'The survival rate is not great. Cord entanglement can happen at any moment.'

Which meant the babies' oxygen could be cut off. Lindsey tapped into her medical knowledge, fearing what Dan was about to tell her. 'Do you want to stop now?'

He gave the ghost of a smile. 'What would be the point? You need to know and, God knows, I need to start gaining some perspective about it all.'

'OK…but I imagine, as a doctor, you knew the scenario you were facing and obviously you tried to shield Caroline about the extent of your fears.'

He dipped his head. How did she know that's exactly how it had been? 'I tried to keep positive for Caroline's sake but it was like living with a time bomb. At sixteen weeks the scan showed they were girls. Their heartbeats were strong and they appeared to be growing well. Caroline was being monitored by an ob team, of course, and they had protocols in place for the babies to be delivered by C-section at the earliest viable date. We dared to hope…' He stopped, his jaw working. 'They died in utero at twenty-two weeks.'

Lindsey heard the pain in his voice and tears welled in

her eyes but she said nothing, just sat with her arms locked around her middle and waited until he carried on.

'We had amazing support from the hospital and my family flew over. And Nathan.' His throat moved convulsively as he swallowed. 'Seeing Nate was hard. Brought it home the reason we were all there. I'd kept it together until then... But I was so damn glad to see him.'

Lindsey felt drenched in emotion, breathing harder as if a thumb pressed on her throat. 'Dan... I'm so very sorry this happened to you.' She looked at him, blinking away the scattering of tears. 'How on earth did you move forward from such heartache?'

'In a fog mostly.' He made an attempt at a twisted smile. 'I'm certainly in no hurry to experience fatherhood again. In the end, you do what has to be done. Caroline didn't want to be around me.' He shrugged. 'She was hurting.'

'And you weren't?' she queried softly.

'Caroline maintained there was nothing holding us together any longer. She quit her job and went home to her parents. I completed my contract at the hospital and then went to Florida. Did some training with a search and rescue team. After that, I came back home to Australia.'

'And you're not in touch with Caroline at all?'

'I tried a few months after I'd got home. She said she'd moved on and she hoped I'd do the same.' He paused. 'It's been two years now.'

Lindsey let the revelation hang for a moment. 'I imagine it's been pretty hard—trying to let it go, I mean.'

'I'm slowly getting there.' He gave a hard laugh. 'Except when it's a significant memory—like on the day I lost it in Resus.'

'I wondered...' She bit her lip. 'You said you were having an off day. But it wasn't the day, was it?' she stated with some perception. 'It was the *date*.'

'Yes, it was,' he said, his voice hollow. 'It was the date I met my babies. And the day I said goodbye to them.'

For a long time they stayed sitting under the tree. Dan had his arm around her, her head buried against him. Finally, he said, 'Thanks, Lindsey—for listening.'

'I hope it helped a bit,' she said, her voice scrappy.

His arm tightened and he pulled her closer.

And he figured only time would tell whether that was true and whether he could start taking more steps forward than backwards from now on.

'Hey.' He gave her a little shake. 'Want to race me home?'

She pulled back. 'I don't know about that.' Raising her arms, she lifted her hair and let it tumble down. 'One of us would probably break our ankle.'

'If it was you, I'd be on hand to patch you up,' he declared manfully.

'Then you'd have to carry me.'

Dan looked unfazed. 'You look like you don't weigh much. I think I could manage to hoist you over my shoulder in a fireman's lift.'

Her mouth turned down. 'I'm too tall for that. I'd be all dangly.'

He gave a deep-throated laugh. 'Dangly you would never be. A gentle jog, then,' he suggested, unwinding upright and taking her with him. 'Let's go.'

When they got home, Lindsey declared, 'You must be starving. What about a club sandwich?'

'Sounds good.' Dan got lemon squash from the fridge and poured them both a tall glass.

Lindsey began setting out the ingredients for their sandwiches. 'Perhaps, later, we could go into Milldale. The country markets are on all day on Sunday.'

'Again, that sounds good. But don't think you have to entertain me, Lindsey.'

She sent him a look of dismay. 'Is that how it seems?'

'Of course not. It's been the most brilliant day I've had in the longest time. And just *being* with you…' He shook his head, still poleaxed by the complete wonder of it all.

'Oh, Dan.' She sent him a misty kind of smile. 'Me too.'

'I think I'll change,' Lindsey said as they finished their impromptu lunch. 'The weather's warmed up.'

'So it has.' Dan hauled off his jumper. He sent her a quick smile. 'Don't be long.'

In her bedroom, she divested herself of her cardigan and T-shirt and stepped out of her jeans. She had managed to hang up a couple of dresses yesterday and she pulled one off its hanger. It was dotted with tiny flowers.

Longish and floaty. I feel like spring, she thought happily.

It was only a ten-minute drive to the village.

'You know, I haven't been to one of these for years,' Dan said as they roamed the market stalls, picking up and putting down various items.

'You should get out more, Dante.'

'Cheeky.' He sent her a lazy grin. 'So, are we looking for anything specific?'

'We are.' Lindsey urged him towards a stall decorated with flags from many nations. 'I like to support this group. They donate to several primary schools in one of the developing countries. Oh, recycled paper!' She pounced on the pale green and speckled box. 'It's Mum's birthday soon, she's a compulsive letter writer. And I must get some of this herbal mixture that helps to heal bruises.'

Dan looked bemused. 'Are you expecting some— bruises, I mean?'

'I work in Casualty, Dan,' she reminded him drily.

'I'm learning so much here,' he said.

Not sure whether he was being serious or not, Lindsey sent him an eye-roll. 'I just need to get some of the fair-trade tea and coffee and I'm done here.'

'I'd like some of that too.' Dan stayed her hand as she was reaching for her purse. 'I'll get this.' He handed over a note of a large denomination, waving away the change.

'That was a nice gesture.' Lindsey swung her carry bag lightly as they strolled on.

'Hardly philanthropic,' he mocked himself. 'But perhaps it might go towards funding some story books for the kids or a bit of sports equipment.'

'Happy thought,' Lindsey said. 'But the hard reality is it might help to pay for someone to keep the kids safe on the way to and from school.'

His mouth tightened at the bleak thought. 'We take so much for granted, don't we?'

'Not always,' Lindsey countered gently. 'I like to think most of us do what we can for others less fortunate. But for some folk it could never be enough.'

Dan looked at her with something like awe. 'You're such a wise woman.'

'So better not mess with me, then.'

He returned her grin. 'I think we need some ice cream.'

'Now let's have a wander through the art gallery,' Lindsey suggested, as they finished off their ice-cream cones. 'Check out the work of the local artisans.'

'Are you among them?' Dan asked.

'I've had a few pieces shown from time to time but nothing lately. I need inspiration.' She paused, her bottom lip puckering, considering. 'Would you sit for me, Dan?'

'No.'

They entered the gallery with its clean lines of black and white space and a striking mullioned window through which the afternoon sun was streaming.

'Just—no?' Lindsey stopped to look at a painting.

'I'm not that narcissistic, Lindsey.'

'That's pathetic reasoning.' She shook her head.

They continued their tour of the gallery and Dan held the door open for her as they left. 'I'd only need you for a couple of hours just to get the basics down,' Lindsey pleaded her case.

'It's not something I'd do. Count me as a firm no!' He softened his abruptness with a smile that spread his lips wide and Lindsey found she was biting down on hers. He looked so sexy, unshaven, a bit rumpled. So...perfect for her.

'Spoilsport,' she muttered, and stepped out into the street again.

Dan wound her fingers through his as they continued up the street. 'I saw a plant nursery when I took a walk yesterday. Would they still be open?'

'Probably. Sunday trading is the go in the village. Lots of tourists about. What do you need a nursery for?'

He squeezed her hand and swung it gently. 'Need to get some flowers for my lady.'

A few minutes later, Lindsey looked at the flowers she held. Dan had given her long-stemmed irises, their colour a rich and gorgeous violet, deepening to amethyst. 'Let's make tracks now,' he said, as they left the shop.

'Thanks for these, Dan,' Lindsey said when they were back and seated in his car. 'But why irises? Any special reason?'

He thought for a moment. 'Because they're extremely special and lovely...like you.' His fingers went to her nape and stroked. 'And brave-looking somehow, with their tall, straight stems.'

She turned to him, her heart beating so heavily she could feel it inside her chest. 'Today's been so amazing, hasn't it?' she said softly.

'Oh, yes…' His mouth lowered to her throat, his lips on the tiny pulse point that beat frantically beneath her chin. He looked at her, an unfulfilled yearning, as sudden as a lightning strike catapulting into his veins. 'I think we need to take this home, don't you?' His voice caught as he swallowed.

She nodded. No further words were needed.

Dan kissed her again before they got out of the car. Then, gathering up their parcels, they went inside. Somehow they found themselves back in the kitchen.

'We seem to end up here, don't we?' Lindsey gave a strained laugh, reaching up for a jug and putting her flowers in water.

'I like kitchens,' Dan said. 'They're friendly places.'

'The hub of the home.' Lindsey felt her nerves jangle, achingly aware of the almost tangible expectation hanging in the air between them. She turned to him, crossing her arms against her chest. 'Tea, then? Glass of wine, anything?'

A beat of silence.

'Dan…?'

He was very close. Unlocking her arms, he slid his hands down to her wrists, holding them gently. They waited there a moment, staring into each other's eyes. He took her wrist and raised it to his mouth. 'We haven't had our dance yet. Do you have some music?'

'I do—heaps of music.' Lindsey felt caught in a bubble. The world had faded and there was just the two of them. She could already feel the surge of heat between them. She swallowed drily.

They went through to the lounge. Lindsey slid a disc into the player and music, slow and smooth, filled the room. She looked up expectantly and saw that Dan had gone to the picture window and was looking out. She crossed to his side and saw what he did. Spears of red and orange shot across the western sky. 'Day's almost done.'

'We still have the night…' His voice was husky on the words as he turned and took her in his arms. Lindsey raised her face for his kiss, her whole body seeming to melt when their lips met. His hands stroked her back, encircled her hips, burning through the soft fabric of her dress as if his fingers were on fire.

Entwined, swaying together, almost lost in the throb of the music, they danced. And danced, wheeling and whirling around the room and all the way down the hallway to his bedroom.

They went in and Dan closed the door behind them. The curtains were partially drawn, the bed turned down. Dan pressed her to his side. 'When did you do this?'

'A bit earlier.'

'For us?'

The softest smile edged her mouth. 'Do you mind?'

He shook his head and paused. 'Ah, Lindsey…'

'What is it?'

'There's no chocolate on the pillow.'

'Silly.' She smiled mistily. 'That's for later.'

At her words, Dan's fragile control shattered and he took her in his arms. Then he stepped back, and without taking his eyes from her face slowly ran his fingers down between her breasts, unbuttoning her simple cotton dress, sliding it in one movement from her shoulders.

Then he was tugging off his own clothes and Lindsey was doing the same. 'This is us,' she whispered, as Dan drew her down with him onto the bed. She wrapped her bare legs around his, her arms reaching up to pull his head down, sighing deeply as she felt the slickness of his skin on hers, felt his body tensing with the effort to control it.

'This is us,' Dan echoed as his mouth ravished hers, hungry, demanding, tasting her everywhere.

Lindsey shivered, inhaling the scent of his naked skin, losing herself, returning his passion with her own kisses, hardly registering when Dan pulled back, pausing to protect her. 'Where were we…?'

'Don't stop…' She held onto him for dear life, his pleasure feeding hers.

Dan had no intention of stopping. Not until he had taken her with him all the way, higher and further, to a place beyond thought or reason. Only when release came, wave flooding upon wave, did they realise how very high and far they had climbed.

Together.

For a long time they lay replete, turned on their sides so they were facing each other. The soft light of early evening fingered the pale walls and ceiling. Outside the window a wood dove called to its mate and a burst of cicada drumming drenched the stillness.

Lifting a hand, Dan lazily combed his fingers through her hair. Something real was happening here. He could do nothing other than feel amazed. 'I'm lost for words…'

Lindsey sighed, sated, wrapping herself around him with the contentment of a purring cat. She gave him an indulgent look from under half-closed lids. She knew exactly what he meant. Freeing a hand, she ran a finger along his jaw and into the slight cleft in his chin. 'I've never wanted to be with anyone the way I wanted to be with you, Dan.'

He felt his heart contract. He could so easily fall for her—if he hadn't already. He could say, *Me too*, and mean it. But it was Lindsey and he needed to spell it out.

He brushed her lips once, twice. 'Without exception, this has been the happiest day of my life. It's been like a day out of time.'

'That's exactly how I feel.' Lindsey stopped and thought.

'It's a pure kind of happiness, isn't it? Like opening a mail-order parcel and finding everything just right.'

He gave a soft chuckle, his breath stirring her hair. 'I'll go with that.' He half spanned her waist with one hand, stroking a lazy pattern on her skin. 'I thought the spa looked pretty inviting earlier. Should we try it?'

'Perfect.' Lindsey rubbed her toes against his in anticipation. 'Then I'll fix us some dinner.'

'Uh-uh.' With exquisite sweetness, Dan claimed her lips. '*I'll* fix dinner.'

CHAPTER SEVEN

'CAN I DO anything to help with dinner?' Lindsey had arrived in the kitchen to find Dan well under way with his meal preparations.

He sent her a very sweet smile. 'A glass of your finest might be the go. I didn't know where to look.'

'Oh, that's easy.' Lindsey went to a door in a recess of the kitchen that led to a proper climate-controlled cellar. 'Red?' she called.

'Mmm, think so. I'm doing pasta.'

Lindsey took glasses and poured the wine and then watched as Dan expertly tossed onions, tomatoes and herbs in a pan. 'That smells wonderful.' She picked up her glass, lacing both hands around it. 'You really do know your way around a kitchen.'

'Would I lie?' He grinned, touching his glass to hers. 'Nathan would have cheerfully existed on takeaways if one of us hadn't cooked. I think he's a bit more interested these days. Sami has probably had some influence there.'

Lindsey made herself comfortable on one of the high-back stools and watched Dan at work. He was such a handsome man. With such an *air* about him. Perhaps it came from good breeding, she pondered. Or from a world of experience in so many ways. Her eyes took their fill. He was wearing a long-sleeved black cotton shirt outside his jeans and he'd shaved.

Her thoughts wandered off, unwinding the last hour. They'd had their spa and then instinctively gone to their separate bathrooms. Lindsey had been glad about that. Her emotions were in overload. She guessed Dan's had been the same. She'd had a long shower and shampooed her hair, spritzed perfume in the air and walked through it. Then, dressed in soft jersey pants and a ruby-red top with a crossover neckline, she'd come to find Dan. She took a mouthful of her wine.

'I took the liberty of lighting the fire in the lounge room,' Dan said. 'OK?'

'Very.' She parked her chin on her upturned hand. Her eyes lit softly. 'There's a little gate-legged table we can set up and eat our meal in front of the fire—if you like?'

'Of course I like.' He picked up his wine, his eyes caressing her over the rim of his glass. 'A perfect end to our perfect day.'

They erected the table and Lindsey set out the place-mats and cutlery.

'We should have some music.' Dan selected something from her collection, flooding the room with rich, mellow sound.

Lindsey was curled against Dan on the sofa. They'd ended their meal with Irish coffee and she'd raided the stash of dark chocolates her mother kept for special occasions.

'Are we fulfilling our brief to just *be*?' Dan smudged a kiss against her temple.

'Passed with flying colours.' Lindsey turned to meet his lips. They were still kissing when the phone rang, startling them apart. 'That's the landline,' she said, levering herself upright. She sent Dan a wry smile. 'Probably Mum from Scotland. She knew I'd be here this weekend.'

'You'll be a while.' Dan got to his feet as well. 'I'll sort this out and start the dishwasher.'

'Thanks.' Lindsey took off down the hallway to the room they used as an office and where their home phone was located. Contrary to what she'd expected, it wasn't her mother at all. 'Oh, Lord,' she murmured, after she'd ended the call and replaced the handset. She had to tell Dan what was happening. Full of misgivings, she hurried along to the kitchen. 'It was Fiona on the phone.'

Dan glanced at his watch. 'At this hour? What's up?'

Lindsey suppressed the urge to run to him. Hold him tighter than tight. 'It's the young couple from the cabin, Scott and Amy. They've just rung Fiona. They don't know what to do.'

'About what?' Dan felt his guts go into free fall. He had a fair idea. And he didn't need this. He really didn't. 'Is it the baby?'

'Amy's waters have broken.'

Dan let his breath out slowly. 'Well, there should be plenty of time to get her to Hopeton. Have they rung for an ambulance?'

'Fiona tried. And they'll get one to us as soon as they can. But there's been a major road trauma twenty Ks out of Hopeton on the Sydney highway, a semi-trailer and two cars. All the ambulances are there.' Lindsey felt her throat tighten. 'Amy's already getting strong contractions.'

In an instant Dan felt as if he was drowning in a sea filled with sharks, waiting to tear him to bits. And there was no escape. He saw the pleading in Lindsey's eyes and turned away, gripping the edge of the bench top until his knuckles turned white. And stared out into the night. He had to get it together. Be professional.

So, sort the logistics. The baby was probably well on the way. They had no history. What if the baby was breach? What if there was a bleed? *Sweet God, he hadn't signed on for this!* He spun back to Lindsey, a truckload of emotions churning through his mind. 'So, where have you left things with Fiona?'

'I've said we'll call her back as soon as we have a plan in place.'

Dan flexed a shoulder dismissively. 'We don't have much choice, do we?'

Lindsey shook her head. If there had been any other way around this, she'd have gone with it. She wouldn't have wished this emergency on Dan for the world. She just had to hope and pray everything would turn out all right for Amy and the baby. And Dan as well.

'The best plan would be to get Amy up here to the house and see what's going on.' Dan's voice was clipped and professional. 'The lounge room is probably the warmest. We'll set up as best we can in there. If you'll call Fiona, I'll get my bag from the car.'

They left the kitchen together, Dan striding ahead down the hallway to the front door.

'I don't suppose you have a birthing kit on board?' Lindsey called after him.

Was she nuts? Of course he didn't have a birthing kit! Without answering, Dan opened the door and stepped out into the crisp night air. He looked up at the tumble of stars and pulled in a deep breath that almost hurt. He had to centre himself.

Or go under.

Why on earth had she asked that damn fool question? Lindsey berated herself. She guessed Dan was feeling hijacked, pushed into a situation he'd rather have avoided. Delivering babies was certainly not on his agenda. And who could blame him?

Dan returned with his medical case and they began getting things ready. The sofa could be converted to a bed. That done, Lindsey went to search for some kind of plastic sheeting, resorting to a roll of garden bin liners she found in a utility cupboard. She came back with her booty plus sheets and cotton blankets. 'Amy could be a bit shocky,' she said, as Dan helped her prepare the sofa bed for their patient.

Well, he knew that. Dan's mouth tightened. Once the waters had broken, many women experienced a kind of delayed shock, shivering uncontrollably. 'I'll stoke up the fire,' he said.

'I'll warm some linen in the dryer,' she said to the back of Dan's head as he hunkered down at the grate. He grunted a non-reply and she shrugged and went off about her business. If the ambulance didn't get here in time…? She felt a curl of unease in her stomach. She'd delivered babies before but not away from the back-up of a fully equipped hospital.

When Lindsey returned to the lounge room, Dan was just putting his mobile away. 'I called Midwifery at Hopeton. Amy's not booked there.'

So no chance of any history. 'Fiona will have an address,' Lindsey said. 'I could check…'

'Bit late for that.' Dan swung round. 'Sounds like them now.' He managed a smile of sorts, softening the tension around his mouth. 'We'll just have to wing it.'

Dan flung the door open. The young couple stood there, Scott supporting his wife. Introductions were quickly made and they were ushered inside. Dan helped Amy onto the sofa bed.

'I feel so c-cold…' Amy was shivering, her teeth chattering.

Lindsey produced one of the cotton blankets warm from the dryer and tucked it over her. 'Try to relax now, Amy.' She placed a hand on the girl's shoulder and rubbed gently. 'Just breathe in and out. That's good.' Lindsey smiled. 'Bit better?'

'Mmm.' Amy blinked rapidly. 'The baby's not due for another three weeks.'

'That's neither here nor there,' Dan said. 'I'm sure your baby will be fine.' And, please, God, able to breathe, he added silently. Don't go there. He clamped his jaw, dragging his thoughts to the present. He turned to Lindsey. 'Could you get Amy ready and I'll see how she's doing.'

Lindsey quickly prepared Amy for Dan's examination. 'Scott, perhaps you'd like to sit over here close to Amy.' She smiled at the young husband, who was looking helpless and overwhelmed.

'We brought the bag Amy packed for the hospital.' Scott looked around awkwardly. 'Where should I put it?'

'I'll take it. And good thinking,' Lindsey said.

Dan bent to his patient. 'I'll be as gentle as I can, Amy.' His examination was painstaking. He was leaving nothing to chance.

'What do you think, Doctor?' Amy bit her lip and grimaced.

'I think your baby isn't waiting, Amy.'

Amy whimpered. 'Scott…?'

'I'm right here, babe.' Scott held tightly to his wife's hand.

Dan took Lindsey aside. 'She's fully dilated and the baby seems small.'

Small? Lindsey felt a lick of unease. 'We're not going to have a problem, are we?'

'Shouldn't think so. Foetal heartbeat is strong. I'd say she's been in labour most of today and not realised it.'

Lindsey stared into his blue eyes. She knew it had probably taken a Herculean effort but he looked in control. Confident. She gave a mental thumbs-up.

'Oh, help,' Amy moaned from the bed. 'I can't do this…'

As if they'd worked together in a birthing suite for years, Dan and Lindsey began talking Amy through each contraction. Dan checked his patient again. 'Not far now, Amy,' he encouraged quietly.

They had only seconds to wait before Amy began moaning again.

'OK, sweetie, big push.' Lindsey helped Amy into a more comfortable position as she bore down, eyes squeezed tight, her fists clenched.

'Head's crowning. We're almost there.' Dan looked down at his hands. The infant's head lay there, streaked and glassy, the dark, perfect curls pressed wetly against the tiny skull. His throat tore as he swallowed. 'Gentle push now, Amy—fantastic. And one more.'

Amy pushed and the rest of the baby slid into Dan's waiting hands. 'You have a daughter.' Dan had unconsciously steeled himself for a baby almost translucent, fragile, but little Miss Fraser was offering up an offended squawk, already pink and beautiful.

'Well done, you,' Lindsey murmured, handing him some cord clamps.

'Did I have these in my bag?' Dan looked bemused.

'Must have.' Lindsey unfurled one of her smiles. 'I didn't find them in the kitchen drawer.'

Dan felt his throat jag again as Lindsey handed him a warm towel to wrap around the infant. He passed the baby to her mother. 'Take great care of her,' he said, his voice not quite steady.

'Nice sound,' Lindsey said a little later, giving a nod towards the top of the bed where the young couple were clucking over their newborn.

Dan refrained from commenting. He felt stretched, hollowed out. 'I'm about to deliver the placenta,' he said. 'Can you find something to bag it? We'll send it to hospital with Amy. They'll need to check to make sure it's complete.'

'Plastic bags I can do.'

Lindsey went along to the kitchen, finding Fiona tip-toeing through the back door.

'Fi!' Her eyes went wide. 'You didn't need to come back. You OK?'

'I didn't like to intrude,' Fiona whispered. 'Is the baby—?'

'Delivered safely. Little girl.'

'Oh, thank goodness.' Fiona put a hand to her heart. 'I felt so responsible for all this. I should have checked how far along Amy was—perhaps recommended they stay closer to the hospital or something...'

'Fi, that's not your brief,' Lindsey said kindly. 'Scott and Amy made their own decision. And fortunately it's turned out fine. Mainly thanks to Dan. He was amazing.'

'Then what a blessing he was here,' the older woman said. 'That both of you were here,' she added, her gaze thoughtful and a little curious. 'Now, should I make some tea?'

'That would be wonderful.' Lindsey searched out the plastic bags Dan needed. 'And some toast as well, please. Amy, especially, must be famished. Oh, do you know if Mum still has Gran's cane-washing basket?'

'Hanging where it always has,' Fiona said. 'On the laundry wall.' She frowned a bit. 'What do you need that for?'

Lindsey smiled. 'It'll make a temporary bassinet for the baby.'

'Oh, bless.' Fiona was almost purring. 'What a sweet idea. Anything else you need me to do?'

'Perhaps you could check on the progress of an ambulance for us. But tell the base everything's under control here so the guys know they're not coming to an emergency.'

Laden with stuff, Lindsey went back to Dan. 'Ambulance has just left Hopeton for us.'

'Good. Placenta's almost out,' he said, continuing to massage Amy's tummy gently.

'As soon as we're finished here, I'd like to give Amy

a little tidy up,' Lindsey said quietly. 'Do you think you could organise a bit of privacy?'

Dan nodded. 'I'll need to write a few notes to send with the ambulance.'

'Use the office,' Lindsey said.

'OK. I'll take Scott with me. That do?'

'Nicely, thanks.'

Her basin of warm water at the ready, Lindsey passed Amy a sponge.

'Oh, that feels heavenly,' the new mother said.

'So, you're not from round here, then, Amy?'

'Further west, Shackleton. Scottie does contract farm work and we have a cottage in town.'

'We'll send you along to Hopeton District when the ambulance gets here,' Lindsey said. 'They'll check you and the baby over and maybe keep you a day or so. Will that suit your plans?'

Amy nodded. 'It'll give Scott time to trade the ute for something more practical for a family before we head home.'

'That sounds like a great idea,' Lindsey approved. 'Now, I'll just raid your case here and get you feeling fresh and beautiful.'

'Come on, let's get this lot cleared away.' Lindsey was looking purposeful. The ambulance carrying Amy and the baby had gone. Scott would follow later when he'd packed up their things from the cabin.

'Damn!' Dan surveyed the chaos in the lounge room and gave a short hollow laugh. 'Do you believe any of this actually happened?'

'Yep.' Lindsey began bundling sheets. 'There's a new little member of the human race to prove it.'

She glanced up. Dan sounded tired and the eyes that lifted briefly to hers were guarded and shadowed. He'd spent the past few hours on an emotional roller-coaster. He must be feeling wrung out.

She made a quick decision. 'Let's leave all this for now,' she insisted. 'Dad usually has some decent Scotch around. Fancy a dram?'

'Lead on.' Dan's agreement was heartfelt.

They were back in the kitchen again, sitting side by side at the breakfast bar. Lindsey had dimmed the lights and the big clock ticked on the wall.

'You're quiet,' Lindsey said as they sat over their drinks. 'You OK?' Her eyes scanned his face, looking for clues.

'I'll do.' He gave a trapped smile. Just, he added silently.

'I'm sorry you had this emergency thrust on you tonight.' Her voice was low, hardly there.

'It was out of your control, Lindsey. Don't stress about it.' He lifted his glass and finished his drink in a couple of mouthfuls.

'Another?' Lindsey offered.

He shook his head. 'I'm good, thanks.'

Lindsey had barely touched her drink. Where did they go from here? she fretted. Where? 'Do you want to…talk?'

'No…not really.' He covered her hand with his. 'Shower and bed, I think.' His eyes locked with hers, dark in shadow, tender in their caress. 'Come with me. I don't want to sleep alone.'

They made love slowly and with great care for each other. The soft mingling of their sighs and murmurs sprinkled the silence until the fire of their passion reignited, driving them before it until there was no escape and they tumbled into a blinding oneness, wrapped in each other's arms.

Lindsey woke to find the room suffused with morning light. At once snatches of their lovemaking flooded her mind and she reached out to touch Dan, but he wasn't there. Her heart fell. Dragging a sheet off the bed, she wrapped herself in its folds and scooted along the hallway to her bedroom. Hastily, she pulled on track pants and a jumper and went to find him.

She headed for the back deck. She had a feeling he'd be there and he was, looking out over the fields, focusing on the clouds of early mist already pierced with gold from the first rays of the sun. He was still. Absorbed.

Almost as if he was looking at it for the first and last time.

'Dan?'

He spun round. 'Hey…'

'Hey…' she echoed. Her eyes widened and she frowned. He was dressed in dark trousers and a charcoal-grey business shirt, his hair still damp from the shower. 'Have you been called in to work?'

'No.' He shook his head. 'Let's sit down. I need to talk to you.'

'OK.' For the first time she noticed his laptop open on the table. They each pulled out a chair and sat opposite each other.

'I'm going to take off,' Dan said bluntly.

'Oh.' Lindsey linked her hands on the table in front of her. He looked jaded, the fatigue lines around his eyes and mouth in sharp relief. 'What's going on?' she asked, her voice catching in her throat.

'I'm flying to Melbourne to see my family—well, my parents at least. I haven't been home since I got back from the States.'

They breathed through a beat of silence.

'You feel the need to be with them,' Lindsey said with some perception.

He was silent for a long moment and then he let his

breath out in a ragged sigh. 'We haven't really had an opportunity to talk properly since the twins... Their grief was as real as mine. They lost their first grandchildren. We need to connect, talk about the babies. Share the loss.'

Which he *should* have been able to do with Caroline. Oh, the unfairness of it all. Lindsey bit hard on her bottom lip. 'Last night...the birth...'

'It sharpened everything all over again. Stuff I'd thought I'd come to terms with—' He stopped, his expression set hard as if anything else would weaken his resolve. 'I'm hoping talking to my parents will give me a way forward. They'll understand.'

Understand, as she'd been unable to. Was that what he meant? She pushed the thought away. 'Would you like me to come with you? Not to your parents' obviously—but just for support?'

He hesitated, as if thinking it through. 'I need to do this on my own, Lindsey. But thanks.'

'When are you going?'

'Soon.' He flicked a hand towards the laptop. 'I'm booked on a flight to Sydney at ten. That'll get me on a connecting flight to Melbourne pretty well straight away.'

And in his mind he was already there, the monumental intimacy they'd shared nothing but a pleasant memory. Lindsey got to her feet, her insides suddenly twisting with the sad truth. 'I'll make some coffee, then.'

'Don't on my account. I'm packed. I should get going.'

She shook her head. 'Why didn't you wake me so we could have had time to talk about this?'

His brows twitched into a frown. 'I'm not following you.'

Damn right you're not.

'You're just...disappearing.'

He looked taken aback. 'With respect, Lindsey, what is there left to talk about?'

Lindsey flinched as though he'd slammed a door in

her face. Suddenly the magic of their lovemaking seemed a figment of her imagination. The carefree, wonderful man she'd discovered had gone. The amazement of their connection all but broken. 'You should get moving, then.'

Lindsey did a frenzied clean of the lounge room after he'd gone. Something in her heart scrunched tight and lodged there. *He should have held me this morning while he told me he was leaving,* she thought sadly. *He should at least have done that. I would have understood. But he'd chosen to walk alone. Well, I don't need you, Dan Rossi.* She kicked the off switch on the vacuum cleaner with the toe of her shoe.

She'd go back to being her own person. Depend on no man for her happiness.

Dan's thoughts were in turmoil as he travelled the thirty kilometres back to Hopeton. He couldn't believe how badly he'd handled things with Lindsey.

He hadn't slept. But that was no excuse for the stuff-up he'd left behind. He could turn round and go back. Sort it quickly. Take Lindsey with him to Melbourne. He glanced at his watch and the faint hope that had flared died. If he did that, he'd miss his flight. And he was pushed for time as it was. He had to be back tomorrow to begin a roster of night shifts.

His thoughts flew back to Lindsey and the way she'd made him feel plain glad to be alive, the way she'd made him laugh. He swore under his breath, disgusted at his lapse this morning. He should have been more caring. But right now talking with his parents had to be his priority. For his own sanity. And if that didn't work, then he had nowhere left to go to feel whole again.

Lindsey spent the afternoon venting her anger and frustration on her clay. She moulded, spun pot after pot and then trashed the lot of them. A bad end to a bad day, she decided grimly, making her way up the stairs from her studio. As she came in from the deck, the home phone was ringing. Dan? Her heart spun out of rhythm and she hurried to answer it, her expectations crashing when the caller proved to be Caitlin Kelly.

'Hey, Lins,' she said. 'I wasn't sure you were still at Lark Hill.'

'I'm taking a bit of leave.' Lindsey perched on the corner of the desk. 'How're you, Cait?'

'Bored.' She gave a half-laugh. 'Actually, I'm driving back to Sydney tomorrow. Wondered if you'd like a change of scene and come with me.'

'To Sydney?'

'Mmm. My apartment's right on the beach at Bondi. It'll be like old times. We could do some galleries for you, some clubs for me and shopping for both of us—are you in?'

Lindsey paused only infinitesimally. To heck with Dan Rossi and his machinations. She owed him nothing. 'You bet I am. What time?'

'Is six too early for you?'

'Honey, I work shifts,' Lindsey pointed out drily. 'My body clock is in permanent disarray. I'll be ready.'

CHAPTER EIGHT

THE FOLLOWING SUNDAY, Lindsey sat up in bed and blocked a yawn. Checking the time, she groaned. It was already well into the afternoon and she must have slept almost the entire day away. But she'd been late home last night, after flying from Sydney then picking up her newly repaired car in Hopeton.

She threw herself out of bed and showered, dressing in jeans and a dark green top. Gathering her hair up, she let it fall haphazardly around her shoulders.

She blocked another yawn on her way to the kitchen, filling the kettle and setting it to boil. That done, she went out onto the back deck.

So much for spring, she decided, leaning on the railings and looking across the landscape, seeing jigsaw pieces of darkening sky between the trees. Unless she was mistaken, those were storm clouds scudding across the mountain-tops as if in a hurry to be elsewhere. But Lindsey knew about these kinds of storms. They came in fast and usually dropped their quota of rain and left just as quickly. She hoped it was one of those but even as she watched, the wind had begun whipping through the trees, swirling their foliage into a mad dance, while a streak of lightning snaked its way across the sky.

Lindsey felt a wave of unease. She'd better prepare in case there was a power cut later. She ticked off her to-do list—first locate the torches, make sure the batteries were viable. She'd just opened the cupboard where the lantern torches were kept when the front doorknocker sounded. Probably Fiona, she thought, come to check she was OK. She hurried along the hallway and opened the door.

'Oh—' Lindsey felt goose bumps break out all over her. Dan stood at the outer perimeter of the veranda, his hands jammed in his back pockets.

'I'm not taking anything for granted,' he said.

Lindsey's fingers tightened on the doorknob. You'd better believe it, she vented silently. Swinging the door wide open, she stepped back and with a small inclination of her head she said, 'Come in.'

For a second Dan's blue gaze faltered. 'Are you sure?'

'Sure I want you to come in?' Lindsey tilted her head in question. 'Of course. Lark Hill welcomes all strangers.'

Dan felt if she had struck him. Was that what he was now? A stranger? Well, he'd asked for it. The lady wasn't going to make it easy.

'I was about to make tea,' she said shortly. 'Come through.'

Dan stepped inside, noticing the carrier bags on the hall table and spilling onto the floor. His eye caught some of the big-name fashion brands, none of which were available in Hopeton. 'Been away?' he asked.

'Sydney, with Cait.' Lindsey sent him a look over her shoulder.

'Good trip?'

'Magic. Cait threw a huge party. Met lots of new people. Just what I needed.'

'Well, that's what holidays are about,' Dan felt compelled to say. But thought darkly that if she was sending a message that she'd moved on and that what they'd had was already history, then he'd got it.

'Looks like a storm coming,' Lindsey said, as she made the tea. 'Are you staying long?'

'Why?' he shot back immediately. 'Do you need to be somewhere?'

Lindsey looked taken aback. 'No...'

Dan's sigh was audible. Lifting his hands, he linked them behind his neck. 'You're still ticked off with me. And I understand that,' he added in response to her elegantly raised eyebrows.

'So at least you agree I have reason to be.'

'I was in overload.'

'And that's your excuse?' Lindsey snapped. 'For the whole weekend we were on fire for each other and then...' She palmed a hand and shook her head. 'You left me feeling...'

'I know... I wanted to turn round and come back but there wasn't time.'

Lindsey felt herself softening. She proffered the mug of tea.

'No tea, thanks.' Dan shook his head. 'I've been on nights. I'm in tea up to the gills.'

Lindsey swallowed. 'Would you like something else, then?'

A tiny pulse flickered in Dan's cheek. 'Just to talk—is that possible?'

She nodded, unable to speak. Every nerve in her body began tightening. What he had to say now would probably make or break them. She flicked a hand towards the kitchen table and they sat facing each other.

'I don't want you to think I'm some kind of messed-up loser.' Without warning his hand reached out and covered hers.

'I would never think that.' Lindsey stared down at the hand covering hers. She took a deep breath and let it go. 'But you do get the prize for behaving with the sensitivity of a block of wood.'

His mouth pulled down. 'Don't hold back on my account.'

'Dan, you all but dismissed me! That was pretty low after everything we'd been to each other.'

He tilted his head back and dragged in air. 'You're right,' he conceded without rancour. 'And I apologise. My only excuse is I wasn't thinking straight.' Abruptly, he pulled away, leaning back in his chair. 'I would never have wanted to leave you feeling hurt and questioning that what we'd had had been anything but entirely special. And *ours alone*,' he emphasised.

Lindsey took a shaky breath and asked the question that needed to be asked. 'Did talking with your parents help, then?'

'Their wisdom astounded me.' His voice roughened. 'I finally realised that I wouldn't be dishonouring my babies if I let them go.'

'Oh...' Lindsey's voice was a thread. 'Oh, Dan...'

'Yeah.' His smile was slightly wry. 'Took me a while to get there. But I have. I hadn't grieved properly. Hadn't said goodbye properly. It was as though there was a chunk of ice inside me that needed to thaw. And it was you who started the thaw, Lindsey. Only you.'

Lindsey's eyes pricked. 'I really just listened.'

'No.' He shook his head. 'You did a lot more than that. You brought something fresh and wonderful to my life. And I realised I had to break out of the mental straitjacket I'd put myself in. That's when I decided that talking to my parents might be the answer.'

Lindsey looked at him earnestly. 'So, what now?'

'For us?' Dan swallowed hard. 'I'd like it if I could hold you, if we could hold each other...'

He'd given her a look so warm Lindsey felt a quicksilver flip in her stomach. She swung up from her chair. 'So why are you still sitting there, then?'

Their kiss started gently but in a second they were desperate for each other. Dan lifted her hair, exposing the side of her throat. Lindsey felt his breath warm against her skin and then came the slight rasp of his tongue.

'Dan...' She gusted his name on a shaken breath and sighed when his mouth felt its way to the corner of hers.

'I've so missed you...' Dan made a muted sound in his throat. It was like the growl of a lion, shuddering through his whole length. 'Missed us.'

'I've missed us too,' she responded, shifting against him, her hands moving in a sweep under his T-shirt, taking him to her.

Where their kisses might have ended, they weren't about to find out. A clap of thunder ricocheted through the house, sending them springing apart. Lindsey put her hand to her heart. 'I don't like the feel of this, Dan.'

'Don't panic,' he said. 'A bit of thunder can't hurt us.'

'It's not that,' she countered. 'Around this valley, it's the wind. It can wreak havoc. The power lines can go down and knock out anything electrical. Is your mobile fully charged?'

He frowned. 'Ah—think so.'

'I'd better call Fiona.' Lindsey took off down the hallway. 'See who's at the cabins.' She was back in a few minutes. 'Thank goodness, there are no guests. The last ones left this morning.'

'One less thing to worry about, then. Do you have torches?' Dan asked.

Lindsey nodded. 'I was about to sort all that just before you arrived.' She got the torches and set them on the kitchen bench, testing them one by one. 'They seem OK.' She looked at Dan. 'When are you back on duty?'

'Late shift tomorrow.'

'So...' She bit her lip. 'You can stay tonight?'

He lifted his hand and stroked his knuckles down her cheek. 'If you'll have me…'

Lindsey pretended to think about it for a moment. 'Oh, I think I probably could.'

'Thank you.' He pulled her into his shoulder for a lingering hug. 'Now, what else do we have to do before the storm hits?'

'Just make sure the windows are secure, I guess. I'm so glad you're here, Dan.' Another crack of thunder sent her snuggling in against him. 'I think I'll make us an early dinner while we still have power,' Lindsey decided. 'Quick frittata, OK?'

'Fantastic. I'm starved. While you're doing that, I'll take a look outside. Might give us a clue if the storm is heading in our direction.'

Lindsey had no doubt it was. She went quickly about her task, sautéing onions, mushrooms and zucchini, fluffing eggs, and scattering fresh herbs and cheese across the top as she poured the mixture into the pan. In two seconds it was under the grill. She raised her eyes in question as Dan came back into the kitchen.

'It's really whipping up a frenzy out there,' he said. 'Actually feels a bit spooky.'

Lindsey punched him lightly on the arm. 'Not scared, are you, Dr Rossi?'

His mouth folded in on a dry smile. 'I thought perhaps you were, Ms Stewart.'

'Milldale girls don't scare easily.'

Dan felt a swell of desire as her lips made a soft little pout. Hell, she turned him on. In a reflex action he swept her up and swung her round and round, ending up in the centre of the room.

'Put me down, Dan,' Lindsey protested, laughing hard and hanging on tightly to his arms. 'That's if you want to eat tonight.'

They ate their meal, one eye on the weather as they glanced up constantly through the big kitchen window. The wind had now begun roaring, the rain falling sleet-like and icy. 'Glad we don't have to go out in this,' Dan said.

'Oh, me too.' Snuggling up in bed sounded like a much better idea.

Dan leaned across, his fingertips making long, shivery strokes down her forearm. 'We have a lot of making up to do, don't we?'

Lindsey made a tiny sound like a purr and felt a strange lightness as if love and desire had rolled into one high-voltage surge, sweeping through her body and out to the tips of her fingers. 'Should we do the dishes?' she ventured coyly.

'Are you serious?' Dan pretended outrage. 'Some matters are vastly more important than others. Don't you agree?'

Lindsey's laughter was sweet and clear. 'I agree.'

CHAPTER NINE

Wednesday, the following week...

FIRST DAY BACK from leave and Lindsey went in to work early.

She hadn't seen Dan since the storm but now she was back in town...the prospect of seeing him every day curved a smile around her lips, a flood of desire pooled into a warm ache inside her. It was a rainy, dreary morning yet she felt she was standing beneath a sunbeam.

It was good to catch up with her team, Lindsey thought as she stowed her bag and finger-waved around the staff lounge. Making a coffee, she joined Vanessa at one of the corner tables that looked out onto a rock garden. This morning the big succulent plants were dewy with rain-drops.

'Well, aren't you the chirpy one?' Vanessa said. 'I take it you had a nice break?'

'Fantastic.' Lindsey's hands spanned her coffee mug. 'But it's good to be back all the same.'

Vanessa gave an eye-roll. 'You *must* be on a high.'

Lindsey laughed good-naturedly. 'How're things with Andrew?'

'I think *cautious* must be his middle name,' Vanessa said darkly.

'Well, he's at a crucial stage of his training,' Lindsey

pointed out gently. 'Perhaps he's not into making commitments just yet.'

'Oh, *yawn*.'

Lindsey gave her contemporary a quick dry look. 'If you think he's worth waiting for, Van, cut him a bit of slack.' She glanced at her watch. 'Who's been the charge on nights?'

'Brooke Bartholomew.'

Lindsey's full lower lip pursed. Brooke was relatively new to the casualty department. She'd seemed nice enough during the casual encounters Lindsey had had with her.

'I don't get her,' Vanessa said frankly. 'She's not on for a chat when things are quiet—well, only with Dan. She kept bringing him cups of tea!'

'Well, that's not a crime.' Lindsey felt a lick of unease she couldn't explain, her pool of happiness shrinking ever so slightly. 'How come you were on nights anyway?'

'Anita Rayburn's little boy was sick. She asked me to swap a couple of shifts.'

Lindsey didn't wait to hear any more. She finished her coffee quickly and stood to her feet. 'I guess I may as well get a jump-start and take handover.'

'OK.' Vanessa helped herself to one of the mini-muffins someone had brought in. 'I'll rouse the team shortly and see you out there.'

'Oh, Lindsey.' Brooke Bartholomew looked up startled from the computer and blinked a bit. 'You're early.'

'I'll take handover, if you like,' Lindsey offered. 'Then you can get off. Are you OK?' She frowned as she looked at the other woman. 'You look a bit rocky.'

'Night shifts…' Brook's nostrils pinched as she breathed in. 'I hate them.'

'Have you been busy?'

'Swamped.'

'Right, who's still waiting for triage?' Lindsey's trained eye flew over the list. One name sprang out and rang warning bells. *Mia Roche*. She turned urgently to Brooke. 'Where is this child now?'

'I was about to get to her. We'd had an MVA and a gunshot wound…'

'Mia Roche is registered at the asthma clinic.' Lindsey was on her feet. 'You should have flagged it.'

'I know. She would have been next. I'll get to her now.'

'No.' Lindsey was definite. 'Page the registrar to Paeds Resus. And, please, Brooke, sign yourself off but don't go anywhere until I've sorted this.' Lindsey's request left no room for argument as she took off at speed to the waiting area. 'Erin!' She located the mother of the sick child and held out her arms for the toddler. 'How long have you been here?'

'A while… I tried to give Mia a drink but she vomited. She's so ill…'

Lindsey could tell that. Mia's little body was radiating heat through her cotton pyjamas. She pressed the back of her hand to the child's forehead, long experience telling her Mia's temperature was far too high for safety. 'Come with me,' she instructed, tight-lipped. With relief she saw her team assembling at the station. 'Vanessa, you're in charge. Jess and Gail, I'll need you both in Paeds Resus.'

Newly graduated, Jess bit her lip. 'I haven't done much paeds.'

'You'll be fine.' Lindsey hardly slowed her stride. 'Gail, you know what to do.' Gail Smith was one of their mature assistants in nursing, an absolute gem in this kind of situation.

The nurses all knew Erin from her attendance at the asthma clinic. Gail placed a guiding arm around the distraught young mother. 'It's OK, sweetheart. Mia's in good hands now.'

Lindsey quickly placed the toddler on the resus trolley. 'Erin, go with Gail now,' she said kindly. 'We'll take great care of Mia.'

'But...' Erin hesitated, her mouth trembling out of shape. 'Shouldn't I...?'

'Best if we leave it to the doctor and nurses now,' Gail said. 'You must be exhausted. Have you been up all night with the bub?'

Lindsey let out a relieved breath as Gail led the young mother from the room. She turned to Jess. 'Get me a Hudson mask, stat. We need Mia on a hundred per cent oxygen. Move!'

Jess moved. 'She's burning up, Lindsey.'

And they were running out of time. They could only hope the little one didn't start fitting. And where was the damned doctor when you needed him? 'Help me hold her, Jess.' Lindsey's calm request held nothing of her inner disquiet. 'I need to get some readings here. Come on, baby, hold still for me,' she pleaded. 'OK, all done... Thanks, Jess.'

'So, we'll give paracetamol next?' Jess had begun to step up into her role.

'Yes.' Lindsey placed what looked like a small piece of dissolvable paper under the little girl's tongue. 'Let's hope it'll start getting her temp down.'

Dan moved at speed through the casualty department. He'd barely pulled into the doctors' car park when he'd been bleeped. And by rights he shouldn't be here at all, but with Martin going home sick he was back on take for the early shift and straight into an emergency.

He pushed through the doors to Paeds Resus. 'What do we have?'

Lindsey spun her head up, expecting to see Martin

Lorimer, and went perfectly still for a beat. 'Dan!' She tamped down a slather of mixed emotions.

He gave a perfunctory nod. 'What do we have?' he repeated.

'Mia Roche, eighteen months old,' Lindsey relayed. 'Ongoing patient at the asthma clinic. Temperature forty-three, oxygen sats seventy-eight, pulse one-seventy. I've given oral paracetamol.'

Deep concern catapulted into Dan's eyes. One glance told him the child was rapidly becoming cyanosed. They'd need to move fast. 'Let's get an IV up and running. Smallest cannula, please, Lindsey. I'll need to crack a vein in Mia's foot.'

They sprang into action, Jess restraining the distressed toddler as best she could while Lindsey assisted Dan.

'Left foot, I think,' he said tersely, gloving quickly. 'I see a vein that might work for us.'

Lindsey's heart twisted. Tiny child, tiny veins. She prayed Dan's skill would be enough. 'I have a cut-down tray ready just in case.'

'We're short on time so let's hope not.' Dan's fingers were deft and sure. He secured the cannula on the first attempt, slapping down a dressing he'd stuck on the back of his left hand in readiness.

'Nice work,' Lindsey murmured, moving in to secure the site with a paediatric bandage.

Dan's expression lightened fractionally. 'Let's run five hundred normal saline and adrenaline five, please. We need Mia on a Ventolin nebuliser. And, Jess, keep checking the sats, please.'

'Yes, Doctor.' After a few minutes the junior reported, 'Sats up to eighty.' Jess looked up hopefully. 'That's a good indication we've got her in time, isn't it?'

Dan looked at the tiny, perfect fingertips. They were beginning to lose their blueness. 'A way to go yet but looking hopeful.' He flicked up his stethoscope. 'I'll have a listen to her chest now. See what that tells us. Left lobe a bit suspect,' he said finally, straightening Mia's little pyjama top. 'She's not allergic to anything, is she?'

'No,' Lindsey confirmed.

'Then we'll start with benzyl penicillin.' He picked up Mia's chart and began scribbling the dosage. 'Plus Maxolon to keep things settled down. Both delivered IV.'

Lindsey prepared the medication, relieved beyond words Mia would pull through this episode and that it had been Dan who had been around to treat this special little girl. Even if he wasn't aware of it, he had a natural affinity with kids. The thought made her happy.

'You did really well,' Lindsey said as she and Jess tidied up. 'Want to debrief later?'

'Thanks, Lindsey. That'd be awesome. Should I get back to the ward now?'

'Yes. Van will have need of you, I'm sure.'

'Excellent work, Jess.' Dan added his congratulations. 'Thanks for your help.'

Jess slipped out.

'I'll hang around until we can safely transfer Mia to Paeds ICU.' Dan pulled up a stool and parked himself beside the bed. 'Parents here?'

'Mum is—Erin,' Lindsey said.

Dan's eyebrows twitched into a query. 'Left it a bit late to bring the child in, didn't she?'

'No, she didn't.' Lindsey felt nettled. 'Erin is extremely up to speed regarding Mia's health. Very unfortunately, triage protocols were not followed here. Mia was kept waiting. I took over as soon as I got in. But I'm going to have to report it to the DON.'

Dan eyed her sharply. 'Who was the nurse on triage?'

'Brooke Bartholomew.'

Dan went very still, all his energies reined in. This

could have dire consequences for the department if he didn't speak up. 'Brooke is battling with some personal issues.'

Lindsey felt wrong-footed. 'How well do you know her?'

Dan hesitated briefly. 'We were thrown together on night shift. She needed to talk so I listened.'

Suddenly the air was taut with tension. 'So, what are you not saying, Dan?'

Dan was quietly monitoring his small patient. 'Brooke spoke to me in confidence, Lindsey. I advised her to ask for a transfer to another department urgently.'

Lindsey frowned. 'If she's not fit to work, she shouldn't be here.'

'You're right.' Dan's look was cool. 'But Brooke was competent on the shifts I worked with her. So what could I do except counsel her to act in her own best interests? Unfortunately, it appears she hasn't. I would have spoken to you about it but you were on leave. So do what you have to do.'

Lindsey shook her head in dismay. She hated having to report another nurse. 'Will you speak with Erin now?'

Dan didn't look up. Instead, he dragged in a weary breath and let it go. 'Yes, of course.'

With Mia finally transferred, Lindsey went back to the station. 'Everything OK here?' she asked Vanessa.

'Everything's under control,' Vanessa said shortly. 'How's Mia?'

'She'll be fine—eventually.' Lindsey paused, swallowing back the swell of emotion that rose in her chest. This was so unlike her. Normally, at work she was clinical and objective. But the thought that things could have just as easily gone drastically wrong for Mia... 'Keep covering for me, please, Van. I need to speak with Brooke.'

'Good luck with that,' Vanessa huffed. 'Don't get me wrong. I feel sorry for her. But the hospital's good reputation could have been put at risk. We all work too hard for that to happen.'

Lindsey's mouth tightened. She'd begun the day with such happiness in her heart. Now she was stuck with Brooke's mess to clean up. She looked at Vanessa. 'I asked Brooke to wait for me. Do you know where she is?'

'She disappeared pretty fast.' Vanessa picked up the phone as it rang. 'Staffroom perhaps?'

Lindsey decided she'd go there first. She just hoped Brooke hadn't cut and run. If only she knew the woman better. And why was Dan suddenly in the mix? she fretted as she pushed open the door to the staffroom. 'Brooke...' Lindsey took a steadying breath. She'd play this by the book. 'Thanks for waiting.'

Brooke took off the black-framed spectacles she'd been wearing and closed the magazine she'd been reading. 'How is the child?'

'She'll recover.' Lindsey pulled out a chair and sat down. 'You know I'll have to report this to the Director of Nursing, don't you?'

'Am I going to lose my job?'

'If there are mitigating circumstances, you won't lose your job. But it's not up to me, Brooke.' During the awkward silence that followed, Lindsey took stock of her contemporary. Brooke had changed out of her uniform into denim overalls and a simple white T-shirt. Her fair hair was out of its knot and flowing freely around her shoulders. She looked curiously vulnerable. 'Is there anything you want to tell me?'

Brooke's chin came up defensively. 'About what?'

'Did you feel ill during your shift? Headache—anything that would have clouded your judgement?'

Brooke worked her bottom lip as if searching for words. Words that wouldn't come.

Lindsey sighed audibly. 'Look, I'll do everything I can to advocate for you. But I'm in the dark here.'

'I was seconds away from getting to Mia.' Brooke tried to justify her actions. 'We were swamped.'

Lindsey kept her cool. 'You were on triage, Brooke. It means you're the first contact. You follow very set protocols.'

'Don't you think I know that, Lindsey?'

'OK.' Lindsey pulled back in her chair and said quietly, 'I'd urge you to be completely upfront with Clarissa. You'll be supported, Brooke, but sadly there may have to be an inquiry.'

Brooke pressed a hand to her temple.

'No one is ganging up on you here,' Lindsey said. 'But we have to follow the rules. Otherwise there'd be chaos throughout the hospital.'

The nurse didn't reply, yet somehow her silence was deafening. 'Are we done now?'

'Yes, we're done.' Lindsey got to her feet. 'Clarissa will be in touch.'

'I'm on days off.'

'But you'll be available on your mobile?'

'Yes.' Brooke stood abruptly. Snapping up her shoulder bag from the back of the chair, she walked out.

Lindsey's mind was churning as she made her way back to the station. As the song said, some days were stones. And today she felt like chucking her job and going to work in the scented serenity of a florist shop. 'Van, a word, please?'

Her friend nodded and came over. 'What happened?' she asked curiously.

Lindsey *tsked*. 'You know I can't talk about that, Vanessa. But I need some air. Can you keep holding the fort for a while longer?'

Lindsey left the hospital by the rear staff entrance. The rain had cleared and the sun was strafing pools of light and warmth across the car park. Leaning against the brick wall, she tipped her head back, breathing in the pure, crisp air. Ah, that felt better. Then she lowered her head and levelled her gaze.

And that's when she saw them.

Dan and Brooke standing beside a silver sports car—obviously Brooke's—their heads very close together, one so dark, one so fair, absorbed in conversation. At least Dan was the one doing the talking while Brooke seemed drawn towards him, her hand on his arm, listening as though her very life depended on it.

Lindsey felt the drum-heavy beat in her chest align with the sudden recoil in her stomach. She dragged in a shallow breath, hurt and anger in equal parts clogging her throat. Not again!

Sick with uncertainty, she spun on her heel and dashed back through the doorway.

Dan found her in the staffroom barely seconds later. 'Lindsey!'

Go away! she felt like screaming as she filled a paper cup at the sink. She took a gulp of water and then turned to face him.

He moved forward, wanting to take her by the shoulders, but caution held him back. Something in her face, her eyes. 'Don't go reading anything into what you just saw in the car park,' he attempted.

Lindsey shook her head. She wouldn't dignify any of this with a response. 'I have no idea what you're talking about, Dan.'

'Look.' Dan spread his hands in a plea. 'It's complicated.'

Lindsey's mouth felt stiff as she took another sip of water. 'What is?'

He frowned. 'Don't pretend you didn't see me with Brooke.'

Lindsey threw professional caution to the winds. 'Don't treat me like a fool, Dan. What the hell are you playing at?'

'I told you before, Brooke is dealing with some personal stuff,' he said, censure in the coolness of his tone. 'She needed a friend.'

'How touching.' Lindsey actually managed a jagged laugh. 'Dan the *go-to* man!'

A muscle at the corner of Dan's mouth pulled tight and flickered. 'This is all a bit juvenile, isn't it?'

'Let's get professional, then.' Lindsey swung round, tossing her paper cup into the bin. 'Are you protecting Brooke?'

'Oh, for God's sake.' In a gesture of a man almost at the end of his tether Dan jabbed his hands to the side of his head and hung on.

'Why can't you give me a straight answer?' Two spots of colour glazed Lindsey's cheeks.

'Oh—hey guys…' Vanessa popped her head around the door, her smile fading as she picked up on the thick tension in the room. 'I was just looking for… Is everything OK?'

'Everything is…fine.' Dan was the first to gather himself.

'Which one of us do you need, Van?' Lindsey swallowed, her throat aching from the brutal exchange with Dan.

'Well, Dan, actually,' Vanessa said carefully. 'We've a two-year-old with an inhaled foreign body. It looks a bit tricky. Andrew would like some guidance. If you wouldn't mind?'

'Where the hell are the paeds people when you need them?' Dan growled.

'Well, we've only one on staff and she's on her honeymoon. There are a couple of others in town but they're in private practice,' Vanessa supplied helpfully. 'No one is conducting a clinic here today. They usually do Monday and Thursday.'

Oh, Van, your timing is appalling, Lindsey gritted silently. Please, just stop the inane chatter and go away.

'Give me a minute,' Dan said. 'Tell Andrew not to do anything until I get there.'

With Vanessa gone, the tense atmosphere heightened again. Lindsey and Dan were left scoping each other. Dan was the first to speak. 'Are you saying I haven't been upfront with you, Lindsey?'

Lindsey felt sick to her stomach. The thought that he might have divided loyalties only increased her unease. '*You* work it out, Dan.'

Tension crackled between them as brittle as spun sugar.

Dan felt his heart surge to a sickening rhythm. God, he didn't want any of this. He felt racked with fatigue, having been dragged back on duty when he should have been on days off. Days he'd been looking forward to when he could spend some quality time with Lindsey after her shifts. Now it was all out the door like the garbage collection. But he had to try to salvage something. 'Look.' He pressed a hand to the back of his neck. 'If this needs to be sorted, let's sort it. But not here and not now. If I can get out of here at a decent hour, I'll come over to your place. And we'll talk.'

Lindsey lifted a shoulder indifferently. She didn't want to be patted down like some kind of recalcitrant child if that's what he was offering. Either they were equals or they were nothing. And right at the moment, she'd put her money on nothing. 'Please yourself.' She walked to the door and turned. She gave a sad little shake of her head. 'I thought I could trust you.'

For a second Dan felt poleaxed. 'You can,' he said. But his words were lost in the vacuum of her leaving.

Working alongside someone you had a personal relationship with was the pits when it all went wrong. Lindsey's throat constricted as she made her way back to the station. Or maybe she was just rubbish at relationships. She looked at the clock on the wall and sighed. It was still hours until the end of her shift.

Dan felt like ramming his fist through the wall. Being at odds with Lindsey felt as bad as having a cartload of gravel dumped into his guts. He swished back the curtains on the paeds treatment room, vowing he would sort things, whatever it took.

The day wore on and Lindsey couldn't believe how bad it felt to be offside with Dan. But there was no going back and she couldn't see a way forward. 'What is it, Jess?' Lindsey looked up sharply as the junior nurse approached the counter.

'Eighty-year-old male, Lewis Gaines,' Jess, who was gaining experience on triage, said. 'He's very frail, seems quite dehydrated and his pulse is thready. I've given him water and told him to keep drinking. But I think he needs to be seen.'

'Let's see what we can do, then.' Lindsey scooted down the list to see where she could juggle patients. 'Is someone with Mr Gaines, a relative?'

'No. He's on his own. He had to come to the hospital on the bus!' Jess was mildly outraged. 'Someone should have cared enough to be with him, Lindsey.'

'In an ideal world, you'd hope so. Right…grab Michelle. She's just back from lunch.'

'Oh. OK.' Jess hesitated.

A jaded sigh left Lindsey's mouth. She knew what this was about. Unfortunately, Michelle had a habit of being offhand with the junior nurses. It left them feeling unsure of their role and devalued as a result. Lindsey realised it was a personality thing with Michelle but they were *supposed* to be a team. 'Take your patient along to cube one, please, Jess, and wait with him. I'll ask Michelle to attend.'

As she made her way through to the cubicles, Lindsey let her pent-up breath go in a stream. It was turning out to be the shift from hell.

It was almost the end of the shift.

'Hey, Lins, want to come for a drink after work?' Vanessa came back to the station and propped herself at the counter.

'Sorry, not today.' Lindsey threw her pen aside and stretched. 'I just want to get home and have a long, long shower.'

'How did your meeting with the DON go?'

'Clarissa took her usual laid-back approach. If Brooke speaks up for herself, it will all probably blow over. I couldn't do anything more than tell it as I found it.'

'You're always scrupulously fair,' Vanessa declared supportively.

'I just want today over,' Lindsey said with feeling. And she still had to deal with Dan this evening. That's if he even showed up.

'Rotten first day back for you,' Vanessa commiserated. 'Why don't I do handover? Then you can take off and get that shower.'

'Oh, cheers!' Lindsey let her shoulders drop as if sloughing off a huge weight. 'That's the best offer I've had all day.'

* * *

Sweet God, how had all this happened? Slumped at his desk, Dan shaded his eyes with his hands. He had to fix things with Lindsey. She was keeping out of his way, delegating the other nurses to assist him.

He was still considering a plan of action when his mobile rang. Sitting back in his chair, he activated the call and then sat bolt upright as he listened.

'You've done what?'

Lindsey's thoughts were deeply focused as she made her way from the station to the staffroom.

'Lindsey…' Dan appeared out of nowhere and closed in beside her.

'Oh!' Lindsey drew to an abrupt halt. She brought her head up in question.

'Martin is back on deck.' Dan got straight to the point. 'He'll be in a bit later. I'll be off duty. We can talk. I'll come to you or we can meet somewhere neutral if you'd prefer.'

There was a wavering in her eyes, a sign of hesitation. Finally, 'My place is fine. Come when you get off.'

Dan felt relief course through him. 'I should be out of here by six. Could I bring a takeaway?'

Lindsey looked up and saw the sheen of appeal in his eyes. 'Thanks, but no need. I'll fix us something. Just one thing, Dan.'

His brow rose briefly. 'Name it.'

'We sort this. Truthfully. No double-talk.'

A tiny pulse flickered in Dan's cheek. His eyes softened, taking in the brave set of her head, the soft curve of her cheek, the sweet, very sweet fullness of her mouth. 'You've got it.'

'Do you have the address?' she asked, almost formally.

'You gave it to me on Sunday night. Remember?'

She did. Soft heat flooded her cheeks. She'd told him when they'd been snuggled up in bed during the storm and she'd foolishly thought that nothing or no one could touch their newfound happiness. Now they were both hurting and she hated it. In a gesture of fence-mending she put out her hand and he took it loosely. 'See you later, then.'

'As soon as I can make it.'

Lindsey couldn't keep still. When would Dan get here? She just hoped he hadn't had an emergency at the last minute. She had her stir-fry ready to just throw in the wok and she'd cooked rice to go with it. Taking a deep breath, she let it go. It felt like a first date all over again. She spun round from the kitchen bench, a little tumble in her stomach as the doorbell pealed.

Dan waited for Lindsey to open the door. Mentally, he was wiped. Today in Casualty had been one that took years from a health professional's life. Add the stress of that to the personal stuff that had gone down…the thought of that made him go cold. Everything between them had so nearly run off the rails today.

Lindsey opened the door. 'Hi…' She met his gaze almost hungrily. 'Come in, Dan.'

He nodded and stepped inside, realising he'd crack wide open if he didn't hold her. Properly. With no agenda. And she had that gleam in her eyes. The one that could send a sweep of sensation down to his toes, igniting all the parts of his body in between. He held out his arms and she melted into them, wrapping herself tightly around him, feeling his chest rise and fall in a broken sigh. 'God, I thought I'd lost you. Lost us.'

She reached up to bracket his face with her hands, her heart in her gaze. 'I hated what happened today.'

'Don't go back there.' Suddenly he looked uncertain. 'Tell me I'm not dreaming. I am actually holding you?'

'You're not dreaming, Dan.' Slowly she became aware of his palm resting warmly at her nape, the tips of his fingers playing gently with the strands of her hair.

'Could we delay *talking* and just go to bed?' he asked throatily. 'I need to put things right.'

CHAPTER TEN

'THAT WAS WONDERFUL.'

'I gathered it must have been.' Lindsey looked on indulgently as he forked up the last of the stir-fry from his bowl. 'You had two helpings.'

'Didn't eat much today,' he offloaded with a grin.

Lindsey looked across at him. 'Today was pretty bad, wasn't it? In all kinds of ways.'

'Just marginally,' he underplayed. 'For most of it I felt as though I had a knife jammed between my ribs. How about you?'

'No knife.' Soft humour shone in her eyes. 'But I wanted to just jump in my car and head back to Lark Hill and never set foot in a casualty department again.'

'That would be a terrible shame.' Dan swallowed the sudden razor-sharp emotion clogging his throat. Today could have all turned out so differently. 'You're an amazing nurse, Lindsey.' His blue gaze shimmered over her face. 'An amazing lover...'

She reached out her hand and they touched fingertips. 'Only with you...'

Her mouth suddenly dried. What they'd found together was still so new. And wonderful. *I think I love you.* Only she didn't voice that thought out loud.

She took her hand back and got to her feet. 'Coffee?'

'Oh, yes, please.' He looked up and thanked her as she took his bowl.

'How long have you had this place?' Dan asked interestedly. They were relaxing on Lindsey's big comfy sofa, their coffee and a plate of orange shortbread, compliments of Fiona, on the low table in front of them.

'I bought it ages ago. When I decided this was where I wanted to be.'

'For always?'

Lindsey looked startled. 'I hadn't thought about it like that. But my job is here. And my family.' She frowned a bit. 'Do you think that's...odd?'

'No.' He gave her a long, intense look. 'Knowing what you want, what makes you happy, sounds wonderfully... grounded.'

Lindsey felt a glitch of uncertainty. 'Not boring?'

'Is that even worth an answer?'

Probably not. 'The house was once a miner's cottage,' Lindsey went on. 'The structure was pretty sound when I bought it and I just refurbished it to my own taste as I went along.'

'You've certainly put your own stamp on it.' He looked around at the unmistakable *Lindsey* touches. 'Some of your work?' he asked, flexing a hand towards the table lamps with their blue and white ginger jar bases.

'Some of my early pieces.' She leant forward and poured their coffee. 'I found the fireplace at an auction. It was in an old post office they were pulling down.' She handed him his coffee. 'I offered twenty dollars to get the bidding started and came home with it.'

Dan gave one of his lazy smiles. 'I'm impressed.'

'You should come with me some time.' Lindsey pressed her head against his shoulder.

'To an auction?'

'I'm guessing you've never been to one. Am I right?'

'Guilty as charged.' His mouth tipped at one corner.

Lindsey took one of the tiny shortbreads and bit into it thoughtfully. 'Are you still in the hospital accommodation?'

'One of the flats. They're not bad and close enough to the hospital to make getting to work on time less hassle.'

'Nathan had a flat there as well, didn't he?'

'Still has. He didn't entirely move out before he and Sami were married. Living there suits me for the present anyway.'

And then what? Lindsey wondered. She knew he had a work contract with the hospital and Dan, being Dan, would honour his contractual arrangements whatever it took. But when his commitment to Hopeton District ran out, then what? Would he go elsewhere? *Then what about us?* she wanted to ask. But couldn't. Possibly because neither of them knew the answer.

Dan's chest rose in a long, uneven breath. The faint drift of Lindsey's distinctive floral shampoo was already escalating into the reality of her head on the pillow beside him earlier. And the completeness of their loving. It came as something of a shock to him that he'd never felt remotely like this before. The thought made him want to go forward with new purpose. Leave no room for doubt or misinterpretation. Lindsey deserved that. He expelled a rough sigh. 'If you're up for it, I guess we should talk about the elephant in the room.'

Well, no second-guessing there. 'Brooke?' Lindsey felt her heart beating in double-quick time. 'I heard back from Clarissa. They had a long talk. At the end of it Brooke decided to resign. She's left the hospital.'

'She's left town as well. She called me.'

So Brooke had his mobile number. Lindsey felt that sense of unease return. Suddenly her nerve ends were tingling, her breathing uncomfortably tight. She lifted her head, searing her gaze with his. 'Is she in love with you?'

'No.' In a kind of releasing gesture Dan raised his hands, ploughing his fingers through his hair. 'It's a bit of an involved story. But now Brooke's gone...' He stopped and considered. 'I don't think it would hurt if I told you. But before I do I want you to know there was nothing going on in the car park when you saw us.'

Lindsey was far from mollified. 'She was practically welded to your groin!'

He gave a reproving look before his mouth twitched into a transparently smug grin. 'I can't help it if women flock round me.'

'Oh, get over yourself, Dr Rossi,' she countered drily. 'I was probably mistaken anyway.' She spread her hands in a shrug. 'Go on with your story.'

Dan looked serious for a moment. 'It's off the record, Lindsey.'

'Of course. And before we go any further, I feel really sorry for Brooke. It was a rotten thing to happen but it did and there were consequences.' When Dan remained silent, she asked, 'Why did she come to Hopeton?'

'Spot on the map,' Dan said. 'As random as that. And there were vacancies advertised at the hospital. It had been a while since she'd nursed but she took a chance and applied. She was offered a position in Casualty. She hadn't wanted to begin there but she needed a job.'

'But it seems as though she was far from comfortable, working there. What kind of training did she have?'

'She was well qualified to work in Casualty. Brooke was in the ADF. She'd done two tours in Afghanistan.'

Lindsey frowned. 'She was an army nurse?'

'She was dedicated. And decorated.'

She blinked uncertainly. 'So, what are you saying?'

'In my opinion, Brooke is suffering from PTSD.'

'Oh—that's awful.' Lindsey felt a flow of sympathy. 'Because of her time in the Defence Force?'

Dan nodded. 'Her fiancé was a soldier. They were both attached to the same company when they were overseas. He was wounded. Brought in when Brooke was on duty.'

'Oh, Lord…' Lindsey squeezed her eyes shut. It got worse and worse. She swallowed heavily. 'Did he survive?'

'No. They airlifted him out but it was too late. Brooke went with him. Not that it counted for much in the end.'

'And Brooke told you all this on night duty?'

'We had long stretches when it was quiet,' Dan replied. 'I'm pretty tuned in to mental fatigue.' He didn't add he'd done advanced training in stress management as part of his search and rescue course. 'I sensed something about her. I put out a few feelers and she responded. I urged her to be upfront with Clarissa and ask for a transfer to another department. Anywhere but Casualty. I think she was getting around to it.'

'But not soon enough.' Lindsey looked thoughtful. 'Did she say what triggered her meltdown this morning? Why she didn't react when Mia was brought in?'

'The ambulance base had called and said there was a gunshot wound coming in. Brooke admitted she freaked.'

Lindsey shook her head. 'Where did all her training go, her protocols?'

'Lindsey, we can't have any real idea of Brooke's mental state at that moment. We hadn't been through what she'd been through. Obviously, she wasn't thinking straight. She spun out at the mention of guns. In any event, it turned out it was only a superficial wound. Some idiot out spotlighting feral pigs had misfired and shot himself in the side of the foot.'

'And in all the carry-on Brooke forgot about Mia.'

'Well—momentarily anyway.'

Lindsey felt her stomach churn. The incident could

have all been avoided if Brooke had just signed off and gone home and let someone else deal with the emergency. 'When did she tell you all this?'

'I watched for her to leave this morning and followed her out to the car park. I reiterated what I'd already told her. Suggested she get counselling as a priority.'

'Instead, she's left town.' Lindsey's eyes looked troubled. 'Where will she go?'

'When she called me she said she was going back to Sydney. She'll have family support there. And I've linked her up with a good shrink. She promised to follow through. Today has been a huge wake-up call for her. She'll get the help she needs now and life will get much better for her.'

'Oh, Dan…' Lindsey scooted up the sofa to him.

'I know.' He gathered her in and placed a soft kiss on her mouth. 'If we all had hindsight, the world would be a much better and kinder place.'

'Brooke kept to herself a lot. It was difficult to offer any kind of friendship.'

'Don't beat up on yourself,' Dan said. 'In our job we can only do what we can do. What people will *allow* us to do.'

'I'll scotch any rumours,' Lindsey promised.

'That'll be good.' He gave her a quick hug. 'You didn't really think I had something going with Brooke, did you?'

Lindsey felt his smile on her skin as he touched his lips to her throat.

'I admit to a smidge of jealousy.'

He looked into her green eyes. An intensity of emotion he'd never felt swamped him. 'You're all I need, Lindsey. So…with that in mind, am I staying the night?'

Lindsey drew in a shaken breath, feeling the sweet sting of anticipation tingle up her spine. 'Where else would you go?' A smile flickered around her mouth. 'But just so you know, I'm on an early tomorrow.'

'Ah.' His eyes caressed her tenderly. 'And I'm on a day off.'

'Then I'll leave it to you to make the bed and tidy the kitchen, shall I?'

He reached out a finger, his touch feather-like along her bottom lip. 'I think I can manage that.'

'Hey, I'm kidding.' Lindsey smothered a laugh. 'I wouldn't expect you to do that.'

'I'll do it anyway.' Carefully, he scooped up a wayward tendril of her hair and tucked it behind her ear. 'I'm really quite house-trained. I thought you knew that.'

'I probably did.' She snuggled closer. 'So, what are you going to do with your day off?'

His mouth quirked. 'I'm going to a talk on beekeeping.'

'Well, that makes sense—not.' Lindsey chuckled. 'Where are you going to do your beekeeping, may one ask?'

He sent her a pained look. 'It's good to have a hobby. And who knows, I may invest in acreage one day.'

Next morning Lindsey drove to work with a new resolve. Surely there had always been a sacred bond among nurses? Perhaps if Brooke had been more open... Lindsey turned into the car park. From today she'd make extra sure her team knew they were valued and supported.

It wasn't long into the shift when Vanessa pounced. 'Did you hear?'

Lindsey lifted her gaze in query. 'If this is about Brooke, Vanessa, yes, I heard. She's resigned.'

'I heard she got the sack.'

'Well, she didn't,' Lindsey said firmly. 'She decided Hopeton wasn't for her and she's gone back to her family in Sydney.'

'Will she be all right?'

'Let's hope so. Brooke was in the armed forces.' Abruptly,

Lindsey decided she'd tell Vanessa just enough to settle the wild supposition that was probably on speaker phone around the hospital already. 'She did a couple of tours in Afghanistan. Apparently, it was pretty rough.'

'Wow...' Vanessa sobered. 'What went down—personal stuff?'

Lindsey nodded. 'Very personal. Someone very close to her was killed.'

'Oh, that's awful.' Vanessa blinked quickly then straightened her shoulders resolutely. 'If anyone starts spouting rubbish about Brooke being sacked, I'll quash it.'

Lindsey's mouth kicked up in a resigned smile. 'Diplomatically, please, Van.'

'Of course I'll be diplomatic.' Vanessa looked wounded. 'By tomorrow it'll all be a non-event anyway.' She picked up the phone as it rang. 'Bound to be something more juicy come along.'

Continuing with her new resolve, Lindsey drew Jess aside when she got a chance later in the shift. 'How did things turn out with Mr Gaines yesterday?' Lindsey knew she could have pulled the notes and found out for herself but it would be helpful for the young nurse's professional development to let Jess debrief.

'Oh, Michelle admitted him,' Jess said earnestly. 'He was exhibiting early signs of pneumonia.'

'So, you made a good call, then.'

'Think so.' Jess's mouth curved, a tiny dimple showing in her cheek.

'Are you getting on all right with Michelle?'

Jess went pink. 'She can be a bit daunting. But yesterday she included me in Mr Gaines's treatment plan and that felt really professional.'

'Good.' Lindsey smiled.

'And Mr Gaines has a nice neighbour who brought some

pyjamas and things in for him,' Jess went on. 'And I got some toiletries for him as well. And some batteries for his little radio.'

'But I hope not out of your own pocket, Jess?' Lindsey pressed the point. Patient care only went so far. And while Jess was very committed to her role, shelling out for patients' extras was not part of it.

'Oh, no. Mr Gaines was very upfront with his money. And Michelle had a chat to him about his living arrangements and apparently his granddaughter from Sydney would like to come and live with him.' Jess continued enthusiastically, 'Grace, that's her name, has a little three-year-old, Liam, and her husband is a FIFO worker. Fly-in, fly-out,' Jess enlarged.

Lindsey hid a smile. 'I know what it means, Jess. So that would seem a good arrangement if they're both keen.'

'Well, Grace is a bit lonely and so is Mr Gaines and he seemed really chuffed to think it might all happen. Michelle's handed everything over to Declan,' she said, mentioning the hospital's social worker.

'Well, good outcome,' Lindsey approved.

'Um...' Jess looked a bit uncertain. 'Is it OK if I run up to Medical to see Mr Gaines now and again? In my break, I mean.'

'Of course.' Lindsey smiled. 'I imagine it would brighten Mr Gaines's day as well. Just realise, though, that in Casualty we're just the jumping-off point. We can't give holistic care, no matter how much we'd like to. You're really enjoying your nursing, aren't you, Jess?'

'More than I thought.' Jess considered. 'And it's nice when your patient says thank you and when you've made a positive impact on them.'

'Perhaps we could nominate you for Nurse of the Year,' Lindsey said teasingly. 'The local Lions Club gives an annual award with a cash prize.'

'Wow—I didn't know that.' Jess's hand went to her heart. 'That'd be so cool—to be nominated, I mean. But I guess one of the midwives would be sure to win.'

'They do seem to have all the fun,' Lindsey agreed. 'Next time we have a staff meeting, I'll run it past the DON.' She touched Jess briefly on the shoulder. 'You know I'm always available if you need to discuss anything work-related, Jess. Or anything personal, for that matter,' Lindsey added, thinking of Brooke again. 'Confidentiality guaranteed.'

'Thanks.' Jess bit her lip. 'Could I extend my time in Casualty, do you think? I really like being part of our team.'

'Just keep doing what you're doing,' Lindsey said. 'That's probably the best way to go.'

Lindsey leaned over the counter to replace a file, deciding that if yesterday's shift had been hell on wheels, today's had been relatively uneventful.

'How was your meeting?' Vanessa looked up from the computer.

'Quick for a change.' Lindsey gave a wry smile. 'Apparently, we're getting a new senior nurse for the department.'

'Mmm, I heard.' Vanessa stretched languidly. 'Charlie Weston, thirty-two, divorced, shared care of four-year-old Poppy.'

Lindsey shook her head. 'You take my breath away sometimes. How do you know all this?'

An imp of mischief danced in Vanessa's eyes. 'Oh, I have my ways. And I like to keep ahead of the game.'

Lindsey cast her eyes down. She wondered how long she and Dan had before their involvement was *out there*. She gave a mental shrug. They'd deal with it when it happened. As it undoubtedly would.

'It's ages since we've had a male nurse in the department,' Vanessa said chattily. 'Do you think he'll come on to our team?'

'We'll have to wait and see, I suppose.'

'We'll lose Annie Logan soon when she takes her mat leave.' Vanessa considered. 'So possibly we'll get Charlie to replace her.'

'Possibly.' Lindsey came round and joined Vanessa at the desk. 'I'll give handover. Take an early mark, if you like.'

'Ta, Lins.' Vanessa was already on her feet. 'I'm off to the gym.' She bit down on her bottom lip around a quick smile. 'Andrew kind of said he might be there.'

Lindsey watched her friend leave. Privately, she thought Vanessa was chasing shadows. If Andrew had wanted a closer relationship with her, he would have acted ages ago, not left her wishing and hoping for something he wasn't capable of giving.

Thank heavens Dan had known what he wanted and gone after it. Lindsey's gaze turned dreamy. She wondered whether he'd be there when she got home. Would he stay again tonight...?

'Afternoon, Lins.'

Lindsey's head swivelled round as charge for the late shift, Greta Ingram, joined her at the desk.

'Oh—hey, Greta.' Lindsey brought her thoughts smartly back to reality.

'How are things?'

'Pretty good, thanks. And with you as well, I imagine.'

Lindsey's eyes opened to questioning wideness.

'You and your new man? I heard you and Dan got off together after Nathan's wedding. Looking very much an item, according to my cousin Alison.'

When Lindsey remained speechless, Greta gave a chuckle and went on. 'You've obviously forgotten Ally works in Nathan's department. Her mum made the wedding cake.'

'Well, I saw Alison there, of course,' Lindsey flannelled. 'But there was a big crowd so I didn't...' She picked up some paperwork and held it against her chest. 'Who else knows?'

'Well, I haven't said anything,' Greta said calmly. 'But would it matter?'

Lindsey thought for a minute. 'I suppose not. You know, in all my years of nursing I've never become involved with someone I worked with.'

'Well, that doesn't make you *odd*!' Greta insisted. 'I didn't date work colleagues either.'

'Kind of ironical then, wasn't it?' Lindsey teased, 'That you actually met your husband-to-be in a hospital setting.'

Greta's husband, Harry, was a painter and decorator. When they'd met, he'd just started his own company and had won the tender to refurbish the entire Hopeton casualty department. 'I thought he needed looking after.' Greta sank onto a chair, looking amused. 'I kept bringing him big mugs of tea.'

'I remember.' Lindsey's laugh tinkled. 'Poor guy. No wonder he was in and out of the men's so much.'

'Oh, he never was!' Greta chuckled and flapped her lanyard in protest. 'Now, what do you have for me?' She moved closer to the computer.

When Lindsey arrived home from work there was no sign of Dan, but he'd left a note on the kitchen counter. It said simply that Nathan and Sami were due back that evening and he was meeting their flight. He'd see Lindsey at work tomorrow.

And he hadn't taken the spare key she'd left him. It was placed pointedly on top of the note.

Now, what was she supposed to read into that? Lindsey fretted as she stripped off and threw herself under the shower. Suddenly her mind was a whirlpool of jumbled thoughts and emotions. Well, obviously Dan didn't trust what they'd found together at all. She'd assumed. And *he* hadn't liked it. Vigorously, she washed her hair and let the shampoo puddle round her feet. Did they have yet another elephant in the room? It seemed so.

As Lindsey towelled dry, she gave a bitter little laugh. Where understanding men and their motives were concerned, she'd obviously been as naïve as Vanessa.

As soon as she saw Dan arrive at work on Thursday morning, Lindsey went straight to his office. There was a knot in her stomach and tension in her muscles as though she'd run a marathon, but she wasn't about to let him retreat to some place in his head and leave her outside.

Knocking briefly on his door, she popped her head in and then the rest of herself. Turning, she closed the door and looked across at him. 'Hi.' She managed a smile. 'Got a minute for me?'

'Of course.' Dan got to his feet slowly, meeting her where she'd stopped at the front of his desk.

He parked himself against the edge of the desk, folding his arms and crossing his feet at the ankles. He sent her a narrowed look, drawn by the intensity of her expression. 'You OK?'

'Fine.' Lindsey shoved her hands into the pockets of her trousers. 'How was your day off?'

'It was good.'

'And the talk?'

'It was interesting.' A tiny flicker of amusement appeared behind his eyes. 'I learned the queen bee mates with fifteen males in mid-air and then flies back to the hive to lay her eggs.'

'Wow! That's quite an impressive gene pool they have going.'

'Mmm.' Dan rubbed his chin. 'I felt a bit sorry for the males, though. They're history after they've mated.'

'That's nature, I guess.' Lindsey hardly gave the statement head room. She had to do what she'd come to do now or let it fester for the rest of the shift. She tilted her head higher and sent him a very frank look. 'So...the key. Too far, too fast?'

He frowned a bit. 'Sorry?'

'I left you a spare key to my home. Clearly, you didn't want it.'

Dan felt the wind taken right out of his sails. He'd hoped for opportunity and the right time to explain his motives but it seemed he wasn't going to get it.

'We hadn't talked about it and I didn't want to presume anything.'

'In other words, you thought *I'd* taken far too much for granted.'

'Hell, Lindsey...' He lifted his hands and scrubbed his fingers impatiently across his cheekbones. 'I don't know what I thought. It just seemed a bit...awkward.'

'Oh, Dan...' Lindsey shook her head. It appeared they still had a long way to go. A long way. 'I left the key as a kind of no-strings invitation,' she flannelled, going all-out to save the situation as best she could. 'I just thought you might have wanted to come back after your talk, relax a bit, even though I wasn't there.' She took a tiny swallow. Even to her own ears the whole scenario sounded less than plausible.

Dan felt the unease in his gut begin to unravel. How had he got it so wrong? Lindsey was everything he'd ever dreamed of in a woman. He'd accepted almost greedily everything she'd offered in the bedroom. Why had he got all stiff-necked about her offer of a damned key! It made his stomach twist. 'I'm an idiot.'

'Well, maybe the jury's still out on that.' She managed a smile of sorts and stepped away. 'Oh.' She turned at the door. 'How were the honeymooners?'

Dan cracked a crooked grin. 'Still in love, by the look of them. They had a great time.'

'Oh, bless. Where did they go?'

'One of the Barrier Reef islands.'

'Fantastic. Ever been?'

He looked a bit sheepish. 'Very remiss of me, I know. Never seemed to get the time.'

'Poor excuse.' Her green eyes lit briefly. 'We'll have to remedy that.'

Why on earth had she made that ridiculous comment? Lindsey gave herself a mental ticking off as she made her way back to the station. The way things were going between her and Dan, they had about as much chance of making a romantic trip to the Reef as being in Edinburgh for lunch on Sunday.

Back at her desk, she buried herself in paperwork.

'You OK?' Vanessa gave Lindsey an assessing look when the two caught up during a quiet moment.

'Yep.' Lindsey gathered her paperwork and tapped it into a neat pile. 'Oh, by the way, Greta left a flyer. Harry and the Rotary need some helpers for a community project. Working bee at the kindergarten. Could you bung it up in the staffroom, please?'

'Sure.' Vanessa scanned the bright yellow notice. 'Oh, it's at the kindergarten that caters for differently abled little ones. I'll be off that weekend, so I'll go along. Perhaps Andrew as well…'

'Did you meet up at the gym?' Lindsey asked casually.

Vanessa made a face. 'He didn't show. I hung around until I'd made myself dizzy on that stupid walking thing. And then I left.'

'Do you think—?' Lindsey stopped. How to be diplomatic here? 'Tell me to mind my own, but do you think it's really working with you and Andrew?'

Vanessa blinked a bit and shrugged. 'Obviously, *you* don't.'

'What do I know about men and their *ways*?' Lindsey snorted.

'Are you and Dan…you know?' Vanessa rocked her hand suggestively.

Lindsey sat back in her chair. Why keep up the secrecy? 'We've been seeing each other a bit.' And wasn't that the understatement of the year?

'You were into something pretty heavy yesterday when I walked in on you.'

'That was entirely work-related.'

Vanessa rolled her eyes. 'And if I believed that, I'd believe someone's just given us the rest of the day off!'

'Oh, hush up, Van,' Lindsey responded mildly. 'It's sorted, OK?'

'You know,' Vanessa said thoughtfully and with a seemingly new-found maturity, 'I'm starting to believe that trying to have a personal relationship with someone you work with is doomed from the outset.'

'Well, perhaps it depends on the *someone*,' Lindsey countered. 'But whatever, it's certainly a minefield,' she added darkly, picking up the phone as it rang. 'MVA coming in. Grab whoever you can and I'll meet you at the ambulance bay.'

He should be certified.

Dan gave vent to a groan of frustration as he drove home. And placed in lockdown, he gritted silently.

What the hell was wrong with him? Why couldn't he just have accepted the key to Lindsey's home with grace? Because deep down he knew it had been a loving gesture from her. And, however much she'd denied it, loaded with expectation. And that fact was what had almost brought him out in a cold sweat.

He made a sound of disgust at his pathetic handling of his relationship with Lindsey. She was lovely, her femininity enthralled him. And she was sweet and clever. And she made him laugh. Put simply so that even an idiot could understand, everything about her called to him. So why couldn't he have sorted things when she'd come to his office? Told her he wanted to take things slowly—for both their sakes. God, after his stuff-up with Caroline—

He shook his head. *But surely to God he could have just taken a step forward and wrapped his arms around Lindsey. Reassured her.*

His jaw tightened, the regret almost numbing him. And he didn't wonder any longer why all day his arms had almost ached with the thought of the lost opportunity.

His introspection was cut short when he responded to an incoming call on his hands-free mobile. 'Rossi.'

'Hey, mate.'

'Nate.' Immediately, Dan's mood lifted. 'How're things?'

'Yeah, great. Are you by any chance on your way home?' Nathan asked.

'Almost there.'

'Any plans for tonight?'

Dan grimaced. He could have had plans but he'd well and truly scuttled those. 'No, I don't have any plans. What do you need?'

Nathan chuckled. 'You know me too well. Actually, I need a hand to shift the last of my stuff out of the flat. Some other dude wants to move in over the weekend.'

'What kind of *stuff* are we talking about?' Dan asked cautiously. 'I don't need extra health cover for a broken back, do I?'

Nathan snorted. 'It's only a few books and things.'

'What books? Those massive medical tomes you've been carting around for years?'

'It won't be that difficult,' Nathan justified. 'I've hired a trolley thing. I just need you and your car boot. It'll be sweet.'

'What's in it for me, then?' Dan shot back.

'Hang on, I'm thinking.'

'Yeah, I can hear the cogs.'

'Fish and chips for dinner,' Nathan offered gallantly. 'Plus a very smooth bourbon.'

Dan cracked a laugh. 'Fair enough. I'm two minutes away.'

CHAPTER ELEVEN

Friday...

CASUALTY WAS BUSY. Lindsey thanked her lucky stars it was. It gave her less time to begin thinking. Analysing. Had she come across to Dan as too organised about their relationship? Too calculating? Pushing too hard? She shook her head. She hadn't meant to give that impression at all.

She wondered how he'd spent last night. Had he stayed home and thought about her? About them? Maybe he'd gone out on the town. Not that Hopeton had much of a night-life during the week but still...

'The police just brought in two old chaps, drunk as.' Vanessa came round the corner of the station and slapped her notes on the desk. 'They politely or impolitely vomited all over the floor and now the waiting room smells like—well, you know.'

'Get the cleaners in,' Lindsey said patiently.

'I tried.' Vanessa's mouth twisted comically. 'They're on a tea break.'

'What's wrong with your patients, besides needing something for their hangovers?' Lindsey asked.

'Cuts and bruises mostly. When the pub shut they spent the rest of the night in the park. A couple of low-lives rolled them this morning. Stole their wallets.'

'What's the place coming to?' Lindsey frowned. 'Are the police looking into it?'

'Dunno. Dan spoke to them.'

'I imagine their ID and social security details were in the wallets.'

'Declan's on it,' Vanessa dismissed. 'For the present, the old boys are *resting* in the side ward. I guess we'll do what we always do. Patch them up, give them something to eat a bit later and send them off.' She flopped into a chair. 'You can't help wondering how people's lives disintegrate so drastically. I mean, they must have been young and hopeful once. I wonder where they'll sleep tonight.'

Lindsey looked at her friend sharply. It was not like Van to be introspective. 'Perhaps Declan will be able to arrange some sheltered accommodation for them. Are *you* OK? You still have some leave due. Maybe you should take it? Get away from the place for a bit.'

'Maybe.' Vanessa managed a jaded smile.

'By the way, Annie finished last night. Her ob wants her to rest up. Our new man is starting on Monday on an early.'

'Oh, joy.' Vanessa brightened. 'On our team, then?'

'For the moment. Uh-oh.' Lindsey sighed as she picked up a call from the ambulance base. She listened to the report and then shot off a few questions of her own. Putting the phone down, she turned to Vanessa. 'Ten girls from St Faith's College coming in from a school camp, suspected food poisoning. ETA twenty minutes.'

Quickly, Lindsey found Dan and relayed the details of the emergency.

'Right, this is where the rubber hits the road, people. We'll need everyone on deck,' Dan said when the team had assembled at the station. 'We'll wait to ascertain the extent of the illness and go from there.'

'And be ready with basins, please,' Lindsey said. 'Some of the students could still be vomiting.'

Within minutes two ambulances had arrived, followed by one of the teachers who had helpfully offered his Land Rover to transport several of the young patients to the hospital.

'Let's get some triage happening, shall we?' Dan came in authoritatively. He half turned his head. 'Lindsey?'

Lindsey ran her eyes over the assembled group. 'This is going to need everyone's co-operation. Some of the students appear quite ill so, Gail, where you can, would you begin taking names, please? And liaise with the accompanying teachers about letting the parents know.'

'How do we work this patient-wise?' Andrew cut in, throwing the question at Dan.

'We'll see the kids on stretchers first. You team with Jess. Michelle, you team with Vanessa. Anything you're uncertain about, don't dither. Give me a yell. Now let's go.'

Accompanied by Dan, Lindsey went into the first cubicle. Their patient, a sixteen-year-old student, looked pale and clammy. Lindsey placed her hand on the youngster's shoulder. 'What's your name, honey?'

'Katherine Enders.'

'And when did you start feeling ill?' Lindsey smoothed the girl's long fair hair away from her cheek.

'Soon after breakfast.' She bit her lips together and went on. 'The other kids were sick too.'

'Katherine,' Dan said gently, 'I just need to feel your tummy.' His mouth compressed as he palpated. 'Right.' He stepped back and drew the sheet up. 'That's fine. Have you had any diarrhoea?'

'Some. Oh…'

Lindsey noticed the girl's sudden pallor. 'Do you want to vomit, Katherine?'

The girl blocked a tear with the tips of her fingers and sniffed. 'I feel so awful.' She swallowed convulsively and tried to sit up. 'My little sister, Alix, is really sick…'

'Shh… It's OK,' Lindsey hushed gently. 'She'll be looked after. Let's just try to get you settled.'

That wasn't going to happen.

'Oh, help!' Katherine gulped and gave a little moan. 'I want to be sick…'

Lindsey grabbed a basin. They were in for a morning and a half with this lot.

'Someone's head should roll over this.' Dan was grim-faced. 'Let's run ten milligrams of Maxolon stat, please, Lindsey. That should settle her nausea.'

Quickly Lindsey secured the drip and taped it down. 'Lomotil for the diarrhoea?'

Dan nodded. 'Start with two orally and cut back to one after each bowel movement. She's dehydrating. I'd like her on four per cent glucose and one-fifth normal saline IV. Sips of water only. Could you take her blood sugar levels as well, please? Anything below three, I need to know.'

And so it went on for the next couple of hours.

'I don't know about you, but I'm starving.' Dan followed Lindsey into the staffroom. They'd just done a round, re-checking all their young patients. And releasing most of them into the care of their parents.

'I have sandwiches, if you'd like to share?' Lindsey offered.

'Hmm…' Dan considered his options. 'I think I'd like something hot. Let's go to Leo's.'

'Oh.' Lindsey hesitated. 'OK. I'll just make sure Vanessa's around to mind the station.'

'What about Alix Enders?' Lindsey asked as they crossed the street to Leo's. 'How long will you keep her?'

'I'd like to leave her drip in a bit longer. She was seriously dehydrated.'

'Did you get any clue as to what may have caused the food poisoning?'

'Probably something dodgy they ate for breakfast, seeing they were ill so soon after. The guys from Health and Safety will suss it out, send whatever they come up with for analysis.' Dan pushed open the door to the café and they went inside.

'I'm not usually out for lunch.' Lindsey took the chair Dan held for her. 'I shouldn't be away from the hospital too long.'

'You're entitled to your break.' Dan had no such qualms. 'And we're only five minutes away if we're needed.'

'I suppose.' She ran her gaze over the short menu. 'I think I'll have the fish.'

'I'll have the beef stroganoff.' Dan placed the menu beside his plate. 'I had fish last night. An impromptu dinner with Nathan and Sami.'

So that's where he'd been. Lindsey looked up as Leo arrived to leave water and take their orders. How pathetic, she berated herself, waiting for any crumb that would let her a little further into Dan's world. While they waited for their food, Lindsey poured them each a glass of water. Suddenly she was aware the silence had extended for too long. 'So... Nathan and Sami settling into their new place all right?'

'New *old* place,' Dan countered drily. 'It's Georgian in design, huge garden, built in the eighteen thirties, according to Sami. She's already on a roll, talking in terms of topiary, stone walling and hedge laying.'

'How's Nathan feel about that?'

'Terrified.' Dan's eyes glinted with soft amusement. 'Sami's been to the historical society to get details of the house as it used to be. She found the front hedge was originally clipped into a whimsical line of marching elephants.'

'Are you serious?' Lindsey spluttered a laugh. 'That girl is totally priceless. But I don't know why I should be surprised. Sami has always known what she wanted and gone after it. I guess that's what Nathan loves about her.'

'I'm sure...' Dan paused. 'Oh, while I think of it, I've been given time off on Monday to attend a refresher training day in search and rescue. If you're pushed, Nathan's back on Monday. He'll come down. And Martin's in at noon.'

Lindsey nodded. 'Thanks for letting me know. Where do you have to go for your training?'

Dan lifted a shoulder. 'Locally.'

And that seemed to be that. Within seconds they were facing another wall of uneasy silence.

It was Dan who broke it.

'Would you like to go out for dinner tomorrow? Perhaps somewhere we could dance as well?' He'd made himself aware of Lindsey's roster, knew she was on an early tomorrow and then off on Sunday, and had decided he could work around that as well.

Slowly Lindsey raised her gaze. Her throat constricted. 'That would have been...good. But I'm heading straight out to Lark Hill after my shift. Mum and Dad are due home next week. I want to make sure everything's looking nice for them.'

It was on the tip of Dan's tongue to ask if she'd like a hand—his for preference—but it was clear she wasn't about to issue an invitation. It was also clear she was making a statement. She didn't want him there. He took a mouthful of water and placed his glass back on its coaster. 'Something's obviously bugging you, Lindsey. Why don't you just hit me with it?'

She didn't pretend to misunderstand him. 'I like clarity in my life. That's how I am. I don't seem to be getting it from you, Dan.'

They stared at each other.

'Let's be frank, then.' Dan's blue eyes glittered. 'You're still ticked off with me because I didn't accept the key you left for me.'

Lindsey hated confrontation but there was no backing down. 'I was hurt at your reaction,' she admitted.

'I acted like a jerk.' His mouth straightened into a grim line. 'Your leaving the key was spontaneous and sweet. I could have called you and sorted it, instead of leaving that pathetic note.' He gave a mirthless laugh. 'God, I can't believe I did that!'

Lindsey raised an eyebrow. 'But you did. And I was left wondering whether every move I make in the future is going to be the right one. If you want out of this relationship, then tell me. Let's end it cleanly.'

End it? Dan felt a cramp in his chest. Was that what *she* wanted? He let his breath go in a stream. He'd been the luckiest man alive, finding Lindsey. Lindsey with the generous spirit, the forgiving heart. But everything had its limits and her patience with him must be running low. 'Are you saying there's no hope for us?'

Lindsey drew back sharply. 'I'm not saying that at all.' She spread her hands in appeal. 'But I can't be myself around you any more.'

Dan felt his heart beating hard against his ribs. 'OK. I hear what you're saying. I don't want to lose you, Lindsey. Lose *us*.'

Lindsey could see the sudden tight set of his shoulders. She didn't want to put pressure on him. Push him to do things he wasn't ready to do. But they couldn't have gone on the way they had been, neither knowing what the other was thinking half the time. 'I don't want to give up on *us* either, Dan.'

'OK, we won't, then.' His blue eyes held an appeal. 'So this is the new, improved me, communicating. If I wouldn't be intruding, I'd like to come out to Lark Hill on Sunday. We could spend the day together.'

'That would be good,' Lindsey said guardedly. 'And definitely a step in the right direction.'

'More like thirty Ks in the right direction.' There was the slightest waver in his eyes. 'So we're back on track, then.'

'Come early on Sunday.' Lindsey tilted her head and reached out a hand across the table. 'I'll put you to work.'

Dan took her hand, shackling her wrist. 'I want to kiss you,' he said softly.

'No chance.' She ran her tongue along her lips. 'Here's Leo with our food.'

'Sunday, then?' Dan leaned back in his chair.

She nodded.

And so it was settled.

They ate quickly and went back to the hospital. As they approached the station Vanessa called out, 'There you are! We've an MVA coming in. Collision between a car and one of those double-cab utilities. Woman reversing out of her gateway into the main road. Guy in the ute didn't have time to swerve.'

'What kind of injuries do we have?' Dan asked calmly.

'Terry Ryan said the woman's pregnant, ten weeks or so. She's a bit shaken but nothing broken. Ute driver's an older man, shocky, possible ribs and seat-belt injury. It happened just out of town a bit so they'll be here directly.'

'Right.' Dan said, 'Anything else happening?'

'No.' Vanessa shook her head. 'We've been quiet.'

'OK.' He glanced at his watch. 'It's nothing Michelle and Andrew can't handle between them. I have a meeting with the board. Lindsey, will you deal?'

'Go.' Lindsey shooed him off. 'Do we have names, Van?'

Vanessa checked her notes. 'Rebecca Brannon and Graeme Ley. Did you have a nice lunch?' she sidetracked deftly.

'Yes, thanks.' Lindsey busied herself at the computer. 'Can't remember the last time I was at Leo's. OK.' She whirled off her chair. 'Van, would you grab Jess and make sure the resus room is ready, please? And check the radiographer's on hand. At some stage there'll need to be an ultrasound done on the pregnant woman.'

'Got all that.' Vanessa took off.

The ambulance siren could be heard outside as Lindsey briefed the junior doctors. She addressed Andrew. 'Which patient do you want?'

'I'll take the ribs,' he said emphatically. 'I've a bit to learn yet about pregnant women.'

'Better smarten up, then, if you're aiming to be a family practitioner,' Lindsey suggested, her tone dry. 'Jess will assist you. Michelle, I'll be with you.'

'Perhaps we should get the ob down?' Michelle looked a question at Lindsey as they made their way to Resus.

'You're the doctor,' Lindsey said. 'It's your call.'

'On the other hand, he'll be grumpy if we call him down for nothing untoward. We'll play it by ear and see how we go, I think.'

Lindsey shot her a discerning look. 'You're OK about treating this patient?'

'Mmm. Yes, of course.' Michelle gave an awkward little laugh. 'I know I've not been the easiest to work with but I'm finally getting the hang of working in Casualty. It's like running a marathon every day.'

'Maybe. But you'll learn a lot here.' Lindsey pulled back the curtain and they went into the resus cubicle. 'Hi, Rebecca, I'm Lindsey. This is Michelle. She'll be your treating doctor. How are you feeling?'

'A bit scared...' Rebecca was shivering, her eyes wide in trepidation.

'Have you felt any bleeding?' Michelle asked.

'No. Don't think so.'

'Well, we'll make sure anyway. Lindsey, would you check Rebecca, please?'

A few moments later Lindsey was able to report, 'So far, so good. But we'll pop a pad on you, Rebecca, so we'll be able to monitor any change.'

Rebecca took a shaky breath. 'I don't want to lose this baby.'

'We'll do everything we can to stop that happening,' Michelle interposed gently. 'Now, I want to check your tummy for any injury from your seat belt.'

Michelle's hands worked their way methodically across her patient's abdomen, palpating, checking and recheck-ing. Finally, she lifted her head and smiled. 'You seemed to have escaped any spleen damage. Now, let's see what the rest of you is doing.' She turned to Lindsey, her brows raised in silent query.

'BP and pulse within normal range.'

'Thanks.' Michelle shone a torch into Rebecca's eyes to check her pupils were normal and reacting. 'OK, that's fine,' she said. 'Now, I want you to squeeze my hand as hard as you can and then I'll check your legs and feet. Ex-cellent.' She smiled. 'You're doing great.'

'Are you ready for the Doppler now?' Lindsey asked from behind Michelle's shoulder.

'We certainly are.' Michelle ran the special obstetric stethoscope over Rebecca's slight bump. For several sec-onds she concentrated, listening. Shifting the stethoscope slightly, she listened again.

'Is s-something wrong?' Rebecca's eyes flew wide in concern.

'Nothing at all.' Michelle gave a reassuring pat to her

patient's arm. 'Your little one's heartbeat is ticking away very nicely.'

'Oh, thank God.' Tears spilled from Rebecca's eyes and down her cheeks.

'Thank you so much, Doctor.'

'I don't think you've anything to worry about,' Michelle said. 'But to make absolutely sure, we'll do an ultrasound as well.'

'Are you booked here to have your baby?' Lindsey spread a blanket over the young woman.

'No…' Rebecca bit her lip. 'I'm from Sydney, here visiting my nanna. It was her car I was driving. It's a bit different from mine. I had trouble adjusting the seat belt and then I think I may have put on too much speed as I reversed. Is the driver of the ute all right?'

'We'll find out for you,' Lindsey said. 'In the meantime, could we contact someone for you—your husband perhaps?'

Rebecca shook her head. 'Dean's away on business. I'll call him later.'

'What about your nanna?' Michelle plonked herself on the corner of the bed.

'She's not been too well. I was actually on my way to get a scrip filled for her.' The young woman gave a funny little grimace. 'She's probably thinking I've gone shopping or something. I…suppose I should let her know…'

'That might be a good idea. I'll speak to her as well, if you like,' Michelle offered. 'Just to reassure her.'

'Thanks…both of you.' Rebecca's eyes flicked between the doctor and nurse. 'For being so kind to me and everything…'

'That's what we do.' Michelle scribbled quickly on her patient's chart. 'Now, if you give me the name of your doctor in Sydney, I'll make sure he or she gets your notes. And I'd like to keep you here for a couple of hours, just to make sure you and your bub are fine. We'll pop you on a saline drip and a little later we'll take some blood. That'll tell us whether your haemoglobin levels are where they should be.'

'OK…' Rebecca pulled herself higher on the pillow. 'Could I have my bag, please? I'll dig out my phone and call Nanna.'

'How's the side ward looking?' Michelle turned to Lindsey. 'Perhaps Rebecca would be more comfortable out there.'

'Should be fine,' Lindsey said. 'Most of our youngsters have been discharged.' She smiled at their patient. 'Now, what about a cup of tea?'

Rebecca gave a little tearful nod of appreciation. 'That sounds like heaven.'

Sunday at Lark Hill…

Hands resting across the railing, Dan and Lindsey were on the back deck, looking down at the patch of newly mown lawn. 'Thanks for doing this, Dan.'

'It's fine.' He sent her a wry smile. 'Anything else you'd like me to do?'

'Well…if you wouldn't mind, I'd like the wood brought in for the fireplace. Even though we're eventually heading into summer, the nights can still get quite cool. Jeff would have seen to all these jobs but he's a bit off-colour at the moment.'

Dan hooked a questioning brow. 'Should I look in on him?'

'Do you have your bag with you?'

'Of course. I'll get it.'

'Dan—stop!' Lindsey smothered an embarrassed laugh. 'I'm kidding. Fiona will have everything in hand.'

'Ah. I see.'

He lifted a hand, stroking the back of his index finger

gently over the curve of her cheek and across her chin. 'You're playing the joker again. Is this something you do only at Lark Hill, Ms Stewart?'

'Must be…' She tried to laugh again but the laughter caught in her throat. His body was very close, his mouth closer still. 'Got you in, though.'

'Payback, then,' he murmured as his mouth came down and closed over her tiny sigh.

While Dan brought in the wood, Lindsey prepared lunch. 'I've made burgers,' she said, when he came through to the kitchen. 'But not your usual kind.' She gave him a quick, hopeful look. 'They're sweet potato and quinoa. And don't look like that.' She flicked him playfully with the tea towel. 'I promise they won't be bland. I've made a chilli yoghurt dressing to go with them.'

Dan washed his hands at the sink. 'So we're on a vegetarian kick today, are we?'

Lindsey put her health professional's hat on. 'It's good to have a change from an all-meat diet.'

'Hey.' He held up his hands in mock surrender. 'Did I say anything to the contrary?'

'No, you didn't.' The dimple in Lindsey's cheek came into sharp relief as she smiled. She loved him like this. Light-hearted. Fun to be with. And the look in those glinting blue eyes sent her insides melting.

They assembled the lunch tray together. 'There's some feta to crumble over the burgers,' Lindsey said. 'Interested?'

Dan's mouth pursed as he considered. 'Think I'll pass. But I'll have some of those black olives, please.'

'And there's rocket from our own veg patch.' Lindsey separated the delicate green leaves from their stems.

'Mmm. Fantastic.' Dan hefted the tray. 'Are we eating on the deck as usual?'

'Why not?' She gathered glasses and a jug of water. 'It's kind of our special place.'

'And I love being here.'

And I love you, he could have added, and wondered why he couldn't voice it.

Because saying it would cause repercussions as wide and deep as the ocean. Was he ready to leave the safety of the shore, take Lindsey with him and set sail to an unfamiliar destination? He deliberately steadied his breathing, tightening his fingers on the edges of the tray and pulling himself back to sanity.

As they neared the end of their informal meal he asked, 'Would you mind if I ran a work-related matter past you?'

'Fire away.' Lindsey refilled their glasses and waited.

'Michelle's evaluation is due. She's about to move on to her next rotation.' He paused. 'Professionally, I wondered how you've found her.'

Lindsey considered her answer. 'Is that a reasonable request, Dan? Michelle's evaluation is surely down to you and Martin.'

'I know all that. But the fact of the matter is the nurses work day in and day out with the junior doctors. And I trust your judgement entirely.'

'Well, in that case...' Lindsey met his gaze, seeing the crease in his cheek as he smiled, the action activating the persuasive gleam in his eyes. 'Michelle's attitude towards the junior nurses has been off-putting for them. They need to gain confidence just as much as the junior doctors do. But things have improved markedly.'

Dan's lips twitched. 'Since you had a quiet word.'

Lindsey gave a shrug. 'She seems to have finally got the message that she's in Casualty as a member of a team. And, believe me, from the nurses' point of view, that's a whole heap of progress.'

'Clinically, she appears very sound. Would you agree?'

'Yes. I've made it my business to work with her a bit more lately. She seems confident in her diagnoses and treatment. And I should charge you for this consult, Dr Rossi,' she added drily.

'Oh, I'll see to it you're well compensated.' His voice was low, deeper than deep, whispering over her skin and right into her heart.

She looked at him mistily. Making love in the afternoon had a lot going for it.

'So, what are you thinking?' Dan's eyes were tender.

'That we have such a lot going for us.'

'We do. I think you're wonderful. And beautiful. And perfect. And damn,' he deadpanned, 'there's my mobile…'

Lindsey sent him an eye-roll, packed up their lunch tray and left him to his call. A few minutes later Dan joined her in the kitchen. He looked serious. 'Everything OK?'

'Hope so. That was the SES.'

Lindsey stopped what she doing and waited for him to explain.

'There's an emergency situation at Mt Rowan. It's near here, I believe.'

'A few Ks up the road. What's happened?'

'Apparently, it's an abseiling group from one of the churches—seven young lads, one leader and one parent.'

'And?' Instinctively, Lindsey moved closer.

'The last of the boys to descend pushed out too far. He came back in at an angle instead of front-on to the cliff and appears to have slammed against some kind of projecting rock. And knocked himself out. Fortunately, his locking device has activated and that's saved him from further injury.'

'Oh, poor kid.' Lindsey looked uncertain. 'But why are the SES calling you?'

'Because I've made myself available this weekend. With my training in search and rescue, volunteering for the SES seems a natural fit. And as I'm relatively close to the accident scene, I said I'd attend. It might be some while before the base can muster a team.'

'Then I'll come with you,' Lindsey said. 'Just give me a minute to change.'

Dan clocked her quick response. 'You're not thinking of abseiling?'

'Of course.' She made a motion of brushing him aside. 'I've done heaps. What about you?'

'As you say. I've done heaps.'

'We're a team, then?'

'We seem to be.' Dan shrugged his acceptance, meeting her hand in a high-five salute. 'Now, get a wriggle on.' He tapped her backside. 'I'll close up the house.'

'Do you have your own ropes and things?' Lindsey asked.

'Yep. Luckily, as I've this training day tomorrow I put together what I thought I'd need for any emergency. See you outside.'

Toby Marshall, the team leader, was waiting for them at the cliff-top. 'Boy, am I glad to see you, Doc,' he said grimly as Dan shook hands and skimmed over the introductions.

'So, do we have a name and how far down is the lad?' Dan asked, already beginning some warm-up arm and shoulder exercises for the physical task ahead.

'Riley Dukes, aged sixteen. By my estimation, he's about twenty metres down.' Toby looked keenly at Dan. 'Obviously he's going to need medical attention, so it's you for the drop, is it, Doc?'

'We'll both go,' Lindsey said firmly. 'I'm a nurse. I'm Dan's back-up.'

'And you've abseiled before?' Toby queried.

'Lots of times.'

'OK, then. The sooner we get this under way, the better

for young Riley. And, Doc, I realise you have your own gear, but I'll need to check what you're wearing. We don't need any more mishaps.'

'Sure.' Dan was compliant. 'No worries.'

'And I'll be your anchor at the top,' Toby said.

Dan showed Toby the special sit-in retrieval harness he'd be wearing, pointing out the sturdy shoulder straps and leg loops.

'You realise you're going to have to attach Riley's harness to yours to get him down?'

'These are the clip gates I'll use for that.' Dan's hands closed around the metal locking devices. 'This type is the best and easiest to operate in case I have only one hand free. And I have a sheathed knife to cut Riley's line away once I have him secured to my harness.'

'Right, you seem well equipped,' Toby said approvingly. 'Don't forget you'll have Riley's extra weight on your line so be aware of the sudden impact when you cut the line away. But I'll have you firmly anchored and it should be fairly smooth sailing down to the base. And hopefully by then the SES team and ambulance will be there. Meanwhile, take this radio. It'll connect you with me. Any problems, yell.'

Meanwhile, Lindsey had climbed into her own harness, tightening the waist belt above her hips.

'You set?' Dan touched her shoulder.

'Yes.' She swallowed the dryness in her throat, checking the trauma kit's bulk, which she'd anchored at the rear just below her bottom. 'Let's do it.' Her eyes met Dan's and clung. She hadn't done this for quite a while, but she wasn't about to tell Dan that. What they had to do would be tricky, to say the least. He would, of necessity, have to keep focused. She didn't want him distracted and worrying about *her* safety.

* * *

Bouncing down the granite face of the cliff, Dan felt the familiar adrenaline kick in. The hard slog of his training in Florida had been well worth this feeling of achievement. Cautiously, he cast a look downwards, just able to glimpse their quarry in his bright yellow sweatshirt. 'We're nearly there,' he called to Lindsey, who was slightly above him and to his left. 'Slacken off.'

'I hear you.' Little by little, Lindsey began paying out her rope, moving on down the rock face until she was alongside him.

'Right—this'll do us.' Dan signalled and together they swung in as closely as they could to the boy. 'And Eureka...' His voice held relief as they landed on a ledge of rock and he began testing its viability. Finally, he managed to position his feet so that he was more or less evenly balanced. 'This should hold both of us, Lindsey. Close up now.'

'I'm with you...' She edged in beside him.

Dan's gaze swung to her. She looked a bit pale. A surge of protectiveness shot into his gut. 'You OK?'

'Piece of cake.' Her brittle laugh jagged eerily into the stillness.

Riley was hanging in space, quite still. But the top part of his inert body had drooped so far forward he was almost bent double into a U-shape.

Dan swore under his breath. Another couple of centimetres and the kid would have turned upside down. They had no time to lose. 'OK, Lindsey, let's reel him in.'

Lindsey looked doubtful. 'Can you reach him from there?'

'Just about, I think. I'll give it a good shot.'

She felt her stomach knot, fearing for Dan's safety as he edged perilously along the ledge, making the most of his long reach to grip the boy's waist harness and guide him in close to the cliff face. Riley's colour was glassily blue. Her nerves pulled even tighter. Were they already too late?

'Lindsey, listen,' Dan instructed firmly. 'I want you to position yourself to receive Riley's torso and support his head, OK?'

Lindsey was put on her mettle. She reached out her arms. 'Right, I've got him!' Immediately, she began to equalise the position of Riley's head and neck, which would automatically clear his airway. 'How's his pulse?'

Dan's mouth screwed tight. 'It's there but it's faint. And no breath sounds. Damn.' He dragged in a huge breath and in one swift movement bent to deliver five quick mouth-to-mouth breaths into their patient.

The silence was deafening; seconds felt like hours as they waited. And then they heard Riley's roughened cough. 'OK, he's breathing but still well out of it. Grab me the torch, Lindsey.' Automatically, he took their patient's weight so Lindsey could access the torch from the trauma kit.

Dan's face was set in concentration as he flicked the light into the boy's eyes. 'Equal and reacting,' he relayed, feeling the tightness in his temples ease fractionally.

So, no bleed to the brain, Lindsey interpreted silently. 'His knee seems at an odd angle.'

'I had noticed.' Dan began feeling around for the clip gates attached to the runner looped over his shoulder. Riley's injured knee was an added complication. The sooner they got the kid down and treated, the better. His gaze lowered to where Riley's injury was just visible below the coloured band of his shorts. The matter of the scraped skin was of little concern but Dan's instincts were telling him that the puffy state of the boy's knee plus the blood seeping from the wound from the rock were a worry. 'He's obviously hit the rock with some force.'

'Do you think he's banged his head and lost control?' Lindsey voiced her own concerns tentatively.

'Quite possibly. Whatever, I can't do much from here.

We'll need to get him down so I can look at him properly. Right, I'm about to try to anchor Riley to my harness.'

Lindsey felt unease crawl up her backbone as she realised the logistics. It seemed a very big ask. Dan was going to try to align Riley's body to his, chest to chest. 'In practical terms, how do you want to work it, then?'

'Slowly and carefully. We'll endeavour to manoeuvre Riley upright now. I'll help as much as I can but I'll have to concentrate on getting him adjacent to my own body so I can link our harnesses together. OK, let's do it.'

It was useless. Lindsey shook her head in despair. It was like trying to steady a ton weight balloon with a piece of string. Riley was a well-built young man, his unconscious state only adding to their difficulties. And in their precarious position, it was nearly impossible to co-ordinate the lift so the two harness belts were close enough to link.

'This isn't going to work,' Dan said concisely. His shoulders slumped and he shook his head. 'This was a harebrained idea.'

Lindsey sensed his anguish but they couldn't give up now. Riley's young life could well depend on their teamwork. She pushed down her fears. 'Give me the clip gates, Dan.'

'That's ridiculous!' His brows shot up. 'Riley's way too heavy and you're not wearing the right kind of harness.'

'I didn't mean I'd try to take Riley's weight,' Lindsey pointed out. 'But we have to find a resolution here. What we're doing is not working—when you're steady, Riley's either too high or too low.'

Dan swore under his breath and slumped into his harness. 'We'll just have to wait until the SES guys get here. They can drop someone. Between us, we'll be able to attach Riley and get him down.' He reached inside his vest for the radio transmitter.

All that could take precious time. Lindsey thought

swiftly. It was time they didn't have. Her confidence in her own capabilities kicked in. 'Wait a minute. Could you try linking your hands under Riley's behind and lifting him to your waist level? Then I could make a grab for his harness and snap you together.'

Dan's jaw tightened so hard it felt like snapping. He hated not being in control. Hated and loathed it. Nevertheless, he did what Lindsey had suggested, gripping Riley and lifting him as high as he could, his muscles straining with the effort.

Lindsey's nerves were stretched like the strings on a bass fiddle. She had only the barest window of opportunity to hitch the two harnesses together before Dan's strength gave out and he'd have no choice but to abort his hold on the injured boy. She steadied her breathing, conscious of almost choreographing her movements.

'Do it now, Lindsey...' Dan gasped, pulling his torso back so Lindsey could use what little space there was between him and the boy. 'Now!' he yelled.

'Do it—or I've lost him!'

In a flash, remembering everything she'd been taught, Lindsey used her feet in a technique called smearing, where most of the climber's weight was positioned over one foot to reduce the overall load on the arms. Twisting slightly, she turned her upper body so that her arm closest to the rock face could counter-balance her movement and give her other arm maximum extension. It took barely seconds to execute.

But to Dan those same seconds felt like hours. The muscles of his throat and around his mouth were locked and sweat pooled wetly in his lower back. His mind was so focused he hardly felt the nudge of Lindsey's fingers as she secured one then two more clip gates to link Dan to his patient.

'Done...' Her voice was barely above a whisper.

* * *

Lindsey hardly remembered how they got down. She only remembered the relief she'd felt when Dan had cut Riley's rope and they'd been able to begin their descent.

And there were plenty of hands to help them once they were safely on the ground. A subdued cheer even went up. Riley was released from his harness and placed on the stretcher.

Lindsey divested herself of her own harness, vaguely aware her legs felt as unsteady as a puppet's. She swallowed back the taste of bile. Surely she wasn't about to disgrace herself and throw up here in front of all these macho men. Someone from the SES handed her a bottle of water. 'Nice work, Lindsey. You're a beauty.'

She managed a weak smile before swallowing several big mouthfuls of water. Her equilibrium steadied and she pulled her thoughts together. Removing her safety hat, she shook out her hair and began making her way across to where Riley's stretcher had been placed in the shade and Dan was bending over him.

Dan looked at her briefly. 'He's come round. You'll be fine, mate,' he reassured his young patient. 'Take it easy now. We'll get you on some oxygen.'

The portable oxygen unit appeared as if by magic. And a space blanket.

'How is he, Doc?' Toby Marshall hovered uneasily. He'd have some explaining to do to the kid's parents over this.

Dan folded his stethoscope away. Riley's breathing was a bit raspy but this wasn't the place to be passing that information along. It would right itself as the oxygen kicked in. 'Riley has a fractured kneecap and possible lower rib injury. We need to get him to hospital.' He turned to the paramedic and took him aside. 'I'll leave Riley in your capable hands, Terry. Cane it in, mate. His parents are probably wearing out the floor in the ED.'

'No worries, Doc. Scratch us a few notes to take and we'll be out of here.'

Late afternoon and the vivid sunset was rapidly being overtaken by the sweep of pearly grey evening sky and the wind that had risen had the sharpness of a whip crack. One of the SES crew had given Dan and Lindsey a lift back to the cliff-top and Dan was rapidly sorting his climbing gear and stowing it safely in his Land Rover.

Arms wrapped around her middle, Lindsey stood watching him. It had been the oddest kind of day.

Dan closed the tailgate on his SUV and turned, his gaze narrowing. He frowned a bit. She looked shattered. 'Why didn't you go and sit in the car?'

'I wanted to wait for you.'

'Aw…' He gave a goofy grin. 'Need a hug, then?' He opened his arms and she ran to him. She cuddled into his embrace and he held her. And held her. 'You were amazing.' He looped back a strand of hair from her cheek. 'I couldn't have done it without you. You had no fear at all, did you?'

Lindsey bit back a snort. If only he knew. But a girl was entitled to warm herself in his male look of admiration for just a little while. 'Climbing is practically a religion around here. We did lots of it when we were growing up and we were taught properly from the beginning. Today was the first time I've had to assist in an emergency situation, though.'

Dan frowned and then said slowly, 'Then I hope you never have to do it again, Lindsey.'

She pushed her hands up under his T-shirt, feeling the

clean sweep of his skin. And loving it. 'I didn't enjoy it much,' she admitted. 'But I was impressed by *your* skills.'

'You were?' His eyes glinted with dry humour. 'You're just saying that.'

Lindsey bugged her eyes at him. 'Stop fishing for compliments, Dante, and take me home.'

'I'm going to have to head straight back to Hopeton, I'm afraid,' Dan said as they neared Lark Hill. 'The training day starts at six a.m. tomorrow.'

'And you need all the sleep you can get. I'm heading back myself. I'm on an early tomorrow and we've a new member of staff joining us. I'd better look at least as though I'm awake and functioning.'

Dan picked up her hand and raised it to his lips. 'I would much rather have lain with you and held you all night.'

'That sounds really poetic…' Lindsey rested her head against his shoulder and smiled. 'Perhaps you do take after your namesake.'

He spluttered a laugh. 'And perhaps not.'

'And here we are,' Lindsey said as they pulled into the Lark Hill driveway and Dan coasted to a stop. Almost simultaneously, they released their seat belts and reached for each other. They kissed long and slowly, savouring every last stroke of the tongue, each lingering taste of each other.

'I won't come in.' Dan pressed his forehead against hers. 'Will you be OK?'

'Mmm. I just have to throw my stuff together and take off.' She moved to open the door. 'Just one other thing, Dan.' She bit her lip. 'I don't know what kind of crazy stuff you'll be expected to do tomorrow. But…please… be safe. For me?'

Dan felt his insides twist, the sudden swell of emotion

hitting him like the force of a king tide. His heart was over-flowing with love for this woman. He reached out, slowly drawing her gaze up so it was level with his. 'I promise I won't do anything reckless. And I'll come back to you safely, Lindsey. For no other reason than I need to.'

CHAPTER TWELVE

LINDSEY LOOKED OUT at the landscape the next morning. It was raining lightly, the gentle, soaking kind that would have the farmers smiling and the mothers of young school children dredging up an endless supply of patience as they pushed reluctant little arms into raincoats.

She pulled a face, making her way slowly from her bedroom to the shower, her leg muscles protesting all the way. So much for the abseiling lark yesterday, she vented silently.

Arriving at the hospital, she went through to the staffroom.

'Well, get you!' From her table near the window, Vanessa looked up, her eyes wide in laughing disbelief. She rattled the pages of Hopeton's daily paper.

'You and daring Dan in a cliff rescue. What else did you get up to, Ms Stewart?'

'Oh, show me.' Lindsey gave a *tsk* and leaned over Vanessa's shoulder to read the report on the incident. 'Why on earth would they have thought this was newsworthy?' she dismissed.

'Because the kid you rescued just happens to be the grandson of Angus Whittaker, the local MP. He was here at the hospital only last week, doing what they euphemistically call "a guided tour". Ring any bells?'

'No.' Lindsey slammed the paper shut. 'He didn't come to the ED.'

Vanessa's mouth turned down. 'Bit too confronting for him, I guess. I heard he went to Midwifery. He wanted to tell them personally he'd got funding for a new birthing suite.'

'Well, bully for them,' Lindsey huffed. 'I could have given him a long list of things we need in Casualty.' She made a cup of tea and came back to the table. 'Riley's surname is Dukes,' she said, wanting to get things straight in her head. 'So his mother must be Whittaker's daughter.'

'Correct.' Vanessa pushed the newspaper aside. 'So, what's to prevent you from popping in on Riley at visiting time? I'm sure his mum would like to meet one part of the rescue team who got her son down from the cliff.'

Lindsey's eyes widened. 'Are you suggesting I should go armed with my list for the casualty department?'

'Well, not quite. But you could start opening doors, so to speak. If you get my drift? I mean, Mr Whittaker's bound to be visiting his grandson some time or other.'

Lindsey grinned. 'You should be working for the UN. But I'll definitely think about popping up to see Riley.'

'Now, what about the second part of my question?' Vanessa wasn't about to be put off.

Lindsey's shoulders lifted in a resigned gesture. There was no use prevaricating. When Vanessa sensed intrigue, she was like a terrier with a bone. 'Yesterday Dan spent the day with me at Lark Hill. He's volunteered for the SES. They called him about the abseiling incident. The rest, as they say, is in the local paper.'

'So...' Vanessa moved her head closer. 'You two are a couple, then?'

'Yes.' Lindsey took a mouthful of her tea and wondered what else you could call it. 'Your hair looks amazing, by the way,' she diverted skilfully.

'Oh, thanks, Lins. Mimi's had a cut-and-colour special.' Vanessa swung her new choppy style as if to emphasise the all-shades-of-blonde highlights. 'I thought I needed an update.'

'Well, it's gorgeous and it suits you.'

A beat of silence and then, 'Oh. My. God.' Vanessa's gaze was riveted on the doorway and the male who hovered there. 'Now, that's what I call a body...'

Lindsey swung round. And blinked a bit. *Wow.* 'That must be our new recruit.' She got swiftly to her feet. 'Let's make him welcome.'

'Wait for me.' Vanessa almost catapulted out of her chair.

'I'm in the right place, then?' Charlie Weston's sea-green gaze tracked between the two women after introductions had been made.

'And on time as well.' Vanessa took the lead cheekily.

'Awesome. I've brought muffins,' Charlie said, with a kind of eager-to-fit-in look.

'Apple and blueberry?' They were Vanessa's favourite.

'Tuna and mustard,' he deadpanned.

'Perfect,' Vanessa shot back, already on the same quirky wavelength. 'Come and I'll show you where to put your stuff.'

Lindsey just shook her head at the pair of them and went to take handover.

When the team assembled, Lindsey allotted jobs, adding, 'Vanessa, I'll leave Charlie's orientation in your capable hands. Yell if you need me.'

'Thanks, Lins.' Vanessa all but batted her eyelashes. 'I'm sure we'll be fine.'

Watching the two walk away, Lindsey noted that Charlie's longish sun-bleached hair was neatly tied back in a ponytail. And she'd already clocked his hands and nails were well kept and scrupulously clean. Good, she thought with satisfaction. He'd do nicely.

By mid-afternoon Lindsey could hardly keep her eyes open. She discreetly blocked a yawn. Yesterday's escapade had obviously taken more out of her than she'd realised. She wondered how Dan was faring.

Dan took some deep breaths, mentally clearing his thoughts for the umpteenth time. He could have done all this stuff standing on his head. But when in Rome…

They'd completed all the physical training and now he just had to sit in on a lecture about handling hazardous materials, dealing with oil spills, chemical leaks and more. Then he'd be out of there. Tonight he and Lindsey were going to dinner with Nathan and Sami. And on Saturday he was going to Lark Hill to meet Lindsey's family. It seemed they were *out* as a couple. Dan was amazed how good it felt.

Friday…

'Are you going to Greta's working bee tomorrow?' Vanessa propped herself on the counter at the nurses' station.

Lindsey glanced up. 'I'll come for a while. Dad's just turned sixty. We're having a celebration dinner for him at Lark Hill.' And Lindsey had invited Dan. It was time he met her family.

'From what I hear, it'll be a good turnout for the working bee,' Vanessa chirped. 'Charlie's coming along too. He's brilliant at DIY.'

Lindsey gave her friend a long look. 'And you know this how?'

Vanessa went pink. 'He's taken over Nathan's old flat. I've been helping him tart it up a bit before Poppy arrives. He's made such a cute job of her bedroom.'

'You and Charlie have really hit it off, haven't you?'

'He's fun.' Vanessa shrugged. 'And I can be myself around him. It's…nice. Uncomplicated.'

And he's so different from Andrew, Lindsey interpreted, happy for her friend. And for Charlie as well, for that matter. Van was a gem.

A week later…

OK, so this was crunch time.

Dan braced himself. He had clearance from the board. He was packed. Now he just had to tell Lindsey. He knew she'd hate it but it was something he needed to do.

He looked at his watch. Still early. But she'd be up and he didn't have much time.

The sound of her doorbell roused Lindsey. She sat up groggily. What the heck?

She sat for a second on the side of the bed and felt around for her dressing gown. Oh, why bother? She was decently clad in long pyjama pants and a T-shirt. Shoving her feet into a pair of slip-on sandals, she clacked to the front door. 'Dan…' She blinked, her gaze uncertain. 'Is something wrong?'

'Morning.' He gave a contained kind of smile. 'Nothing's wrong. May I come in?'

'Of course.' She stood back to let him in.

'Did I wake you?' He looked concerned.

Lindsey finger-combed a fall of hair from her forehead. 'I'm on a late. I just felt like a sleep-in. Come through. I'll make some tea.'

'I'll make it,' Dan offered.

He felt guilty. She looked whacked.

'Thanks.' She gave a wry smile. 'I'll wash my face and wake up a bit.'

After she'd changed into jeans and combed her hair, she felt more in control, more like herself. She headed into the kitchen, where Dan was making himself busy.

'So, what's up?'

He handed her a mug of tea and she saw he'd made toast as well. She took long mouthfuls and looked at him above the rim of her mug. Waiting.

'I have something to tell you.' Dan was hunched over his tea mug.

She forced her lips into a smile that felt stiff and uncomfortable. 'Better get on and tell me, then.'

Dan hesitated as if searching for the right words. 'Have you been watching the TV news at all over the last twenty-four hours?'

She shook her head. 'Why, have I missed something important?'

'A category-three cyclone has hit parts of New Guinea's coastline, and particularly a little island to the north. It's called Cloud Island. There's huge damage and their resources are poor. The ADF are organising to send supplies and personnel as we speak. They need MOs on the ground. I've volunteered. I'm flying out at noon today.'

'Oh.' She moistened her lips and took a long controlling breath. 'How dangerous will it be?'

Dan shrugged. 'It's hard to put a classification on it at this stage. But there'll be protocols in place. We'll just follow orders mainly and do what we're trained to do. In my case, I'll be helping to set up a field hospital and treat the incoming casualties.'

Her throat closed tightly. 'Are there many people injured... do you know?'

Possibly hundreds, he could have told her, but refrained. 'Well, the gurus at the weather bureau are calling it a natural disaster so I imagine there'll be a bit of tidying up in all directions.'

'How long will you be gone?'

'Don't know yet. Possibly not more than several weeks. Once the hospital is up and running, the army will start taking things over, bringing in more of their own personnel. But right now they need as many trained boots on the ground as they can get.' A muscle pulled in his jaw. 'And I *am* trained for this kind of emergency, Lindsey. I can't just sit on my hands and do nothing.'

Her heart did an odd tattoo. One part of her was inordinately proud of him but the other part... She looked at him, her eyes unguarded. 'I guess there's nothing to say other than take care of yourself.'

'Of course I will.' Dan reached out and took her hand across the table. 'You take care as well while I'm gone.'

She gave a jagged laugh. 'I'll be just going to work and coming home. I can't get into much trouble.'

'Will you come out to the airport and see me off?'

Lindsey stared at him for a moment, then suddenly and clearly, saw things from his perspective. He had to go. And she was glad and proud of his humaneness and the depth of his commitment to medicine and his willingness to use his skills in whatever way and wherever they were needed. 'Of course I will.'

'You're not taking much.' Lindsey saw he had only a carry-on bag. They were in Hopeton's airport lounge and holding hands tightly.

'We'll be issued with everything. I'll try for a video hook-up so you can see me in my army fatigues.'

'And handsome as all get-out.' Lindsey tried to joke but it was hard. She swallowed. 'So when you get to Sydney, what then?'

'I'll meet up with the rest of the contingent. We'll fly out in a Hercules later today, I imagine. Look at the TV

news tonight. There's bound to be a camera or two record-
ing our departure. I'll send you a wave.'

'And I'll be bound to see it,' she said drily, looking out
through the glass wall of the passenger lounge to the air-
strip, where the luggage was being ferried across for load-
ing. She felt a wrench to her heart. He'd be gone soon. The
line of her mouth trembled for a second.

Watching her, Dan took stock, finding it hard to believe the avalanche of emotion that swamped him. He,
Dan Rossi, had fallen headlong in love with this beautiful woman. And what he had to say couldn't wait a moment longer. 'I love you absolutely, Lindsey Stewart. Will
you marry me?'

Dazed, her mouth opened and closed. She couldn't
speak. She just bit her lips together and nodded. Then
smiled as if her lips might crack. 'Oh, Dan...'

'So that's a *yes*?' Dan's eyes locked with hers.

'Yes! Of course, yes! I love you, Dan. How could you
think I didn't?'

Dan's heart began clamouring. He heaved in a long
breath and let it go. Joy, clear and pure, streamed through
him. Oblivious to the crowd around them, he pulled her
close and kissed her—hard. 'When?'

Lindsey felt shaky and happy all rolled into one. She
fiddled with the button on his shirt front. 'As soon as you
like. As soon as you come back from your tour?'

'Yes.' He nodded eagerly. 'In the meantime, think about
what kind of wedding you'd like and I'll do the same. And
we'll do it,' he added softly, as if making a promise to himself, a promise to both of them. His eyes clouded for a second. 'And you don't mind all my baggage?'

She placed her fingers on his lips, her gaze clear and
untroubled. 'What baggage? This is *us*, Dan.'

He took her hands and held them against his chest, as if
reaffirming their commitment. 'It's about time I got that

into my head. After I get back, I never want to be away from you again.'

'You won't have to be,' she said, knowing it as surely as she knew her own name. 'We'll be together.'

'Oh, my Lindsey…' Dan leaned into her, kissing her softly, tenderly.

'This is the best day of my life.'

Lindsey's smile was tremulous. 'And mine. Oh.' She lifted her head and listened. 'That's your boarding call. Do you have everything you need?'

His face worked for a minute. 'Everything but you.' He gave her one last, fierce kiss. 'That'll get me through the tough times,' he said, and picked up his bag.

Lindsey watched as he jogged across to join the end of the queue of boarding passengers. Suddenly, he turned. He began walking backwards and smiling. 'I love you!'

'And I love you,' she echoed, but he was already out of sight.

Two weeks later…

'Have you heard from Dan recently?' Vanessa asked as she and Lindsey met up in the staffroom before work.

Lindsey made a face. 'The mobile reception is pathetic. I've had a few phone calls. But Dan said the army techs are hoping to have a satellite up and running shortly so that will make communication easier.'

Vanessa propped her chin on her hand. 'You look a bit wan, Lins. You're really missing him, aren't you?'

Lindsey nodded and bit her lip. 'Every day seems like a month.' She paused. 'Dan asked me to marry him as soon as he gets back.'

Vanessa's mouth fell open. 'Get *out*. Oh, Lins—that's amazing! And you said yes? Of course you did. Oh…' Vanessa's hand went to her heart. 'A wedding. How could you have kept that kind of news to yourself? I'd have been doing a shout-out all over the ED. What plans have you made?'

'Well, none, really.' Lindsey was still feeling stunned to some extent. She needed Dan's presence to make things real.

'I'll help you,' Vanessa said promptly. 'We'll make a list. All you need is the date, time and venue. And your dress, of course. And the guest list. Oh, and flowers…'

Lindsey managed a shaky laugh. 'I need to think about it a bit more, Van. But thanks.'

Vanessa batted a hand. 'What kind of wedding does Dan want?'

'We left it open-ended. We'll decide on something when he gets back…'

'But you could get a jump-start,' Vanessa pointed out excitedly. 'Guys usually go along with whatever the bride wants anyway. I'll dash out on my break and get the latest bride books. Lace is so *in*. But you'll look stunning in whatever you wear,' she summed up happily.

Lindsey locked her arms around her stomach. Butterflies as big as doves were looking for a place to land. Vanessa's enthusiasm had been like an avalanche, drowning her in excitement. And the faintest trepidation.

Later in the day, Lindsey was surprised to receive a phone call from Sami.

'Is it OK to call you at the hospital?' Sami asked.

'Of course.' Lindsey swung away from the computer. 'If I'm elsewhere in the department, you can always leave a message and I'll get back to you. Is everything OK?'

'It's wonderful.' Sami gave a throaty laugh. 'Look, Lins, I know Dan is away and you're possibly a bit at loose ends so I wondered if you'd like a little catch-up after work— cup of tea or something?'

'What a good idea. That sounds just what I need. Where?'

'You know where my cubbyhole is in the main street? There's a tea room newly opened a few doors down. It's called Browne's. I'll pop along and keep a table. See you when you get there. All right?'

'Fantastic.' Lindsey smiled, glad for once she'd brought a change of clothes to work.

'Over here!' Sami's blond curls bobbed as she waved Lindsey across to the table. The two friends hugged briefly and settled themselves in the old-fashioned high booth. 'Now, what are we having?' Sami scanned the menu. 'Pot of tea?'

'Oh, yes, please!' Lindsey smiled and ran her tongue along her lips. 'I'm parched.'

'And something to go with it…' Sami made a moue of conjecture. 'Everything looks a bit buttery and I'm so off sweet stuff. What about cucumber sandwiches?'

'Lovely.' Lindsey tossed back her head and laughed. 'We can pretend we're having high tea at the Ritz.'

Sami cackled. 'Have you done that too?'

'A long time ago with James and Catherine.' Lindsey looked up as the waitress arrived to take their order.

'So, what news do you have for me, Lins?' Sami asked, placing the menu back in its folder.

'Dan's asked me to marry him,' Lindsey blurted. Once she'd told Vanessa, she'd been bubbling with a queasy kind of happiness all day.

'He did?' Sami gave a subdued squeal. 'That's brilliant!' She pressed her hands together in a praying motion under her chin. 'Oh, help… I feel a bit teary. Dan's so lovely. And you're so right for each other. So, are we invited to the wedding?'

'Of course, you dope.' Lindsey blinked a bit and thought

she may as well start making concrete plans. 'In fact, I wondered whether you'd be my matron of honour...'

'Absolutely! I'd be delighted. As long as it's relatively soon so I'll fit into my dress.' Sami's look grew misty. 'I'm pregnant, Lins...'

It was Lindsey's turn to look stunned. The outline of Sami's face went out of focus and then righted itself. 'Ooh...' She let her breath go in a sigh. 'That's so sweet. Congratulations!'

'Thanks. It's a bit sooner than we planned but...you know?' Sami looked coy.

Lindsey felt her own tears welling up. 'I'm so thrilled for you and Nathan. Are you feeling OK healthwise?'

'Pretty good, actually. Off the sweet stuff, as I said, but so sleepy I can't believe!'

Sleepy. Lindsey's stomach heaved alarmingly. Warning bells like the peal of a carillon resounded in her head.

'Mum said she could fall asleep at the drop of a hat when she was expecting Cait and me,' Sami went on happily. 'I've been so looking forward to getting our house in order and now we've a nursery to plan. And Nathan's on cloud nine. He'll be such a *dad.*'

It can't be. Lindsey clasped her hands on her lap, then unconsciously spread them over her tummy. *I'm imagining things. I have to be.* She'd had a period. But it had been lighter than usual. Much lighter, she corrected. It didn't mean anything untoward. She lifted her cup and swallowed a mouthful of her tea. She had to leave. But she couldn't, not yet. Instead, she half listened to Sami. Gave answers when she had to and Sami was on such a roll she hardly noticed anything amiss. Except when they got up to leave.

'You know, Lins, you're looking pale. Working in that hospital environment does absolutely nothing for your complexion.'

Lindsey laughed the comment away and felt as though her lungs had flown into her throat. Sami blew air kisses and they parted, promising to meet again soon.

As Sami had said, they had dresses to choose and a wedding to plan.

Would there even be a wedding now? Lindsey felt shaky as she reversed out of the parking bay. She'd go to one of the busy big chain pharmacies where no one would recognise her and buy a pregnancy testing kit. She swallowed. It was absolutely the last thing she'd expected to be doing when she'd got up this morning.

When she arrived home, she went straight through to the bathroom. Removing the box from the chemist's wrapping, she felt as though she was handling a time bomb.

And it may as well be. An explosion that would surely blow her and Dan's plans for their future to smithereens. He'd said that after the tragic outcome with his twins he was in no hurry to experience fatherhood again. She couldn't do it to him. Present him with a fait accompli like Caroline had done. No way I'll do that to Dan, she vowed, preparing herself for what she had to do.

The test was positive.

Lindsey felt all the strength drain from her legs as she sank down on the side of the bath. *I'm having a baby.* We're *having a baby.*

She sat there for a long time. Then, surprisingly calmly, she got up, had a shower and shampooed her hair. Out of the shower, she towelled dry and dressed in a pair of her softest cotton pyjamas, then went through to the kitchen and put the kettle on. She gave the ghost of a smile. Perhaps she'd have to stop drinking so much tea. She called in sick for work next day. She needed time to herself. Time to start planning hers and her baby's future.

Next day...

Lindsey was amazed she'd slept so soundly but as the day wore on she was aware of a slow crawl of panic overtaking her. She so wished Dan was there so she could have told him, got everything over and done with. And if he walked, so be it. She'd manage on her own. She could even go to Scotland, to James and Catherine. Have her baby there. Her thoughts flew wildly ahead.

The ringing of the doorbell startled her out of her introspection. She sighed, hoping it wasn't Vanessa with her wretched bride books! She went to the front door, flinging it open almost impatiently. And took a breath so deep it almost hurt. 'Dan!' She'd already begun steeling herself for when he'd get back, running over little speeches in her head, but seeing him standing there in the flesh, still dressed in his army fatigues, all her carefully prepared words flew away like leaves in the wind. 'When did you get back?' she croaked.

Dan gave the briefest smile. 'Flew into Sydney in the early hours this morning. Had to hang about for a debrief. There wasn't a flight to Hopeton until God knows when, so I got a cab.'

'You got a cab from Sydney!'

'Needed to see my girl.' He followed her inside to the lounge. 'I rang the hospital. They said you were home sick so I came straight here.' His gaze flew over her. She certainly looked under the weather, not like his bright, beautiful Lindsey at all. And surely she'd lost weight in the time he'd been gone. He put out his hands and took hers. 'Are you actually sick?'

'No—not really.' Just *worried* sick more like. 'I felt like a day to myself, that's all.'

'Ah.' His eyes burned like brilliant sapphires. He grinned. 'Well, you won't be getting that now, will you?'

Suddenly, like a dam breaking, Lindsey burst into tears.

'Hey…what's up?' Dan guided her down onto the sofa. Hell. He felt his heart beating hard against his ribs. What was wrong here? He held her until at last she took several shaky breaths and regained control.

'Oh, Dan…' She curled her face into his neck.

'It'll be OK, Lindsey.' He stroked her back. 'I love you. Whatever it is, you can tell me.'

That's just it, she thought despairingly. I don't know how to.

'Have you gone off me?'

'What?' That brought her to her senses in a flash. 'Of course not.' She sniffed, reaching for the box of tissues on the coffee table. 'This is so unlike me.' She gave a watery smile and made use of the tissues.

'Better now?' His eyes were so close she could see the faint specks of silver in the blue.

She nodded.

'OK, then.' Dan stretched his arm along the back of the sofa behind her. 'I can't keep guessing, Lindsey. Just spell it out. Please.'

His voice was gentle but it couldn't free her from the stomach-caving fear that this was all too difficult, and even now, when he'd told her he loved her, she still couldn't guarantee his reaction would be one of…gladness?

His fingertips stroked the back of her neck. 'I'm going nuts here, sweetheart. What the hell is it?'

Lindsey drew in her breath and let it go. 'I'm pregnant. We're having a baby.'

A beat of silence, absolute and prickling with awareness and disbelief.

A baby. Dan felt his heart double in size. For a second he felt his life spinning out of control and then it slowed and came right. And he was able to think. 'We always used protection.'

'Well, we obviously slipped up. It happens.'

Another beat of silence.

'Have I ruined your life?' he asked quietly.

Lindsey looked at him uncomprehendingly.

'Do you want to be pregnant?' he asked in the same quiet manner.

She jerked upright. 'Are you asking if I want your baby, Dan? *Our* baby? Perhaps I should be asking you if you want it. Because if you don't—'

His kiss cut her off. Rough. Then gentle. Sweeter than sweet. She felt his chest rise and fall in a broken sigh. 'Give me a break, Lins. I think I'm in shock. But I also think I'm ecstatic.'

'Really?'

'Did you think I wouldn't be? Our own baby.' His hand smoothed over her tummy as if he hoped there might already be changes. 'When did you find out?'

'Just yesterday.' She went on to tell him about Sami and Nathan's news and how she'd identified with some of Sami's symptoms.

Dan chuckled. 'Nathan a dad! What a stud, eh!'

Lindsey slid her hands around his neck. 'Our babies will grow up together. Won't that be a laugh?'

He pressed a kiss into her hair. 'What about you? Are you feeling all right?'

'Think so,' she murmured.

'Do you have an ob you prefer?' Dan's mind skipped to professional matters.

'Therese Gordon.' She paused. 'And don't take this the wrong way, Dan, but I don't want you hovering.'

'Oh.' Dan felt his throat suddenly dry. A thousand reasons why he *should* be hovering juxtaposed in his head. And who could blame him—after last time? But there was nothing to indicate that Lindsey's pregnancy would be anything but perfectly straightforward. He had to get that through his head. 'OK.' He took a deep breath and let it go. 'I promise I won't be neurotic about things. But I would like to be there for your scans and ultrasounds.'

'And I'll *want* you there,' Lindsey hastened to reassure him. 'Like any normal expectant dad.' She brushed a kiss across his mouth. 'I love you, Dan, but this is *us*.'

And thank heaven for that. Mentally, Dan kicked all his uncertainties to oblivion, resolving to leave them there.

Lindsey snuggled closer. 'I'm so glad you're back.'

'Me too.'

'How was it?'

'A bit taxing but we managed. Things are quickly getting back to normal. That's why they chucked out the civilians and got their own medics in. Have you thought what you'd like for our wedding?'

'Sorry, no.' She ground her bottom lip. 'I just couldn't seem to get my head around it and then when I found out about the baby...'

He cupped her face in his hands. 'Surely you didn't think I'd do a runner?'

'I hoped not...' She took a deep breath. 'Prayed not. But you were adamant about not wanting fatherhood again.'

His gaze deepened and darkened. 'I was still angry back then. And I hadn't realised I'd just met the love of my life.' He shook his head as if it still amazed him. 'Could we pull a wedding together pretty soon?'

Lindsey looked into his eyes, seeing the sheen of tenderness. 'I think we could. But we'll need a licence.'

He tapped his breast pocket. 'I already have one. Picked it up in Sydney this morning. It's amazing how fast you can get things done when you're in uniform.'

'Oh, Dan,' Lindsey chided. 'Did you let them think you'd been posted?'

He shrugged. 'I suppose I might have given that impression. I just looked a bit helpless and they fell over themselves cutting red tape.'

Lindsey fisted him on the chest. 'You couldn't look helpless if you tried. But back to the wedding. Where? Any preference?'

'Lark Hill? That's if it's all right with your folks. Something intimate and all about us. What do you think?'

'That sounds perfect. There's a wonderful spot amongst the vines where we can make our vows. Reception up at the house. We don't want a crowd, do we?'

He shook his head. 'Just your lot and mine, a few mates from the ED and Nathan and Sami to stand up for us. Easy. Can you take a couple more days off?'

'I guess so. What do you want to do?'

'I still have a few days' leave up my sleeve. I'd like us to fly to Melbourne tomorrow so you can meet my family. We'll take them all to dinner and you'll be wearing your ring.'

'Oh…' Lindsey reached out and placed her palm against his cheek. 'Are you buying me an engagement ring, then?'

'Absolutely. And we'll get matching wedding rings as well.' He smiled indulgently. 'I want to do things properly.' He added silently, this time.

CHAPTER THIRTEEN

A few weeks later, Saturday, a wedding at Lark Hill...

IT WAS MID-MORNING and a clear day. A bridal path had been especially prepared between the rows of vines.

A string quartet was playing softly.

Surrounded by a stunning display of old-fashioned bush roses and fruiting vines, Dan was waiting with Nathan. The guests were seated in bespoke chairs. It was an informal setting but the atmosphere was laden with dignity and purpose. And so much love for the happy couple.

Vanessa sat with Charlie. They were now officially *going out*. Or staying in, as Vanessa laughingly told anyone who would listen. Poppy was now living with her dad most of the time. She adored Vanessa and the feeling was mutual. Charlie leaned over and whispered, 'Is my tie all right?'

Vanessa gave it a quick straighten. 'It's fine. Why?'

'I looked everywhere for it this morning, then found Poppy had been using it as a lead for her guinea pig.'

Vanessa rolled her eyes. 'Why didn't you just wear another one?'

Charlie looked blank. 'I don't have another one.'

'Shh...the music's changing. The bride must be on her way.' On cue, the guests rose as one. Vanessa gripped Charlie's arm. 'Oh, bless...doesn't she look gorgeous? I

knew she'd wear lace. And look! Dan's going to meet her.
Oh…it's just too romantic.'

Daintily, Vanessa began tapping away the press of
happy tears.

Charlie, wearing a goofy grin, handed her his big red
hanky.

The newlyweds stepped into their reception, where the atmosphere was already bubbling with laughter and music.

'Dr and Mrs Rossi,' announced Nathan, who was dou-
bling as master of ceremonies.

'I like the sound of that.' Dipping his head, Dan kissed
his bride gently but thoroughly for all the world to see.
'You take my breath away, Lindsey Rossi.' His eyes held
a gleam of teasing humour. 'I'm so glad you turned up
this morning.'

Lindsey gave a shaky laugh, her heart cartwheeling
with happiness. 'Of course I turned up,' she countered.
'This is our party. Our beautiful wedding day. Doesn't
everything look amazing, Dan?'

It did.

The lovely old home was adorned with fresh garden
flowers and a sumptuous buffet lunch was set out on the
long table in the dining room. There was comfortable seat-
ing everywhere. Guests could wander out to the verandas
or into the garden. The back deck had been cleared and the
floor sanded and polished for the dancing later.

Lindsey directed Dan's attention to their wedding cake,
lavishly decorated with meringue buttercream icing and a
trail of blue forget-me-nots. A silver-spangled bauble on
the top declared simply: *Love*.

'This is Fiona's gift to us.'

Dan looked smug. 'I knew she approved of me from
the get-go.'

They wandered out onto the deck, where so much of

their courtship had taken place. Dan lifted Lindsey's hand and kissed her fingers and the sunlight caught her new rings, causing a beautiful rainbow of sparkles to reflect all around them. 'I love you,' he said for the umpteenth time. 'What about dancing with me?'

Lindsey looked at him through a haze of happiness. 'I think we're supposed to wait until after the speeches and we've cut the cake.'

Dan looked unimpressed. 'It's our wedding, we can do what we like.' He spun her away and she sashayed back to him, draping her arms around his neck.

His eyes lit with satisfaction. 'Happy?'

'I am.' Lindsey smiled serenely. 'You're a very nice man, Dan Rossi.'

Dan gathered her closer. His beautiful Lindsey had come to him today as his bride. He had no doubt their marriage would be good and true. He had to be the happiest man alive.

'And not a bad dancer,' he said.

EPILOGUE

'PANT THROUGH THE BREAK, LINDSEY,' Jenna Metcalf, the midwife, coached.

'I can't…'

'Yes, you can,' Dan encouraged.

'The lights are too bright,' she whined. 'Dan…?'

'Head's almost out,' Jenna said. 'One more push…'

'One more push,' Dan echoed. 'Come on, Lins, he's almost here.'

Lindsey gave a long sound of effort, one that thrust her head back hard against Dan's chest as he held her. They wanted pushing? Well, she'd give them pushing!

'That's it. You're amazing.' Dan kissed the top of her head. And prayed as he'd never prayed before.

'Gently now. Almost there,' Jenna called encouragingly. 'Looking good. Head's out. I'm delivering one shoulder. Wow.' She laughed. 'We have a strong little guy here. He's very anxious to meet his mamma and daddy, aren't you, gorgeous?' In seconds, she held the baby up, his little body all wet and slippery.

Dan made a noise that came from deep within his chest. *Born.* Their son was safely born. His eyes stung and filled as baby Rossi cried lustily and waved tiny fists.

'Oh, Dan, look…' Lindsey's voice cracked. 'He's so beautiful. And perfect.'

'Perfect,' he whispered throatily. Almost in a daze he

cut his son's umbilical cord. 'Jen, thank you.' He felt his throat clear and he swallowed. 'You were brilliant.'

'Uh-uh.' Jenna shook her head. 'Your wife was the brilliant one.' She expertly wrapped the baby and handed him to Lindsey.

Dan moved to sit beside Lindsey, his whole heart in his eyes. 'Put your hands beneath mine,' she said, pressing her cheek against his shoulder. 'And we'll both hold him.' She smiled mistily. 'He looks like you.' Gently, she unwrapped their infant son and they looked in wonder at the perfection of his tiny limbs, fingers and toes. 'Happy?' Lindsey looked at Dan, knowing how special this moment was for him.

Dan nodded, too full for any words—well, any that would make much sense. He felt a surge of love and protectiveness for his beautiful Lindsey and their little boy. They were a family. They had been truly and magnificently blessed.

Lindsey stroked the gentlest finger around the baby's cheek, watched as his little mouth moved instinctively in a suckling motion. Tipping her head back, she smiled at Dan and their gazes locked in sweet understanding.

Lindsey placed the softest kiss on her husband's mouth and then bent to look again at their son. Pride and a kind of triumph filled her. 'This is *us*,' she said.

* * * * *

If you enjoyed this story,
check out these other great reads from
Leah Martyn

WEDDING AT SUNDAY CREEK
REDEEMING DR RICCARDI
DAREDEVIL AND DR KATE
WEDDING IN DARLING DOWNS

All available now!

MILLS & BOON®

THE ULTIMATE IN ROMANTIC MEDICAL DRAMA

A sneak peek at next month's titles...

In stores from 26th January 2017:

A Forever Family for the Army Doc – Meredith Webber

The Nurse and the Single Dad – Dianne Drake

Just can't wait?
Buy our books online a month before they hit the shops!
www.millsandboon.co.uk

Also available as eBooks.

7/03.2

MILLS & BOON®

EXCLUSIVE EXTRACT

Kate Ashton's night with Sam Ryder leads
to an unexpected consequence—but can he
convince this nurse that their love is meant-to-be?

Read on for a sneak preview of
THEIR MEANT-TO-BE BABY
by Caroline Anderson

'You didn't tell me you were a nurse,' Sam said.

'You didn't tell me you were a doctor.'

'At least I didn't lie.'

Kate felt colour tease her cheeks. 'Only by omission. That's no better.'

'There are degrees. And I didn't deny that I know you.'

'I didn't think our...'

'Fling? Liaison? One-night stand? Random—'

'Our private life was anyone else's business. And anyway, you don't know me. Only in the biblical sense.'

Something flickered in those flat, ice-blue eyes, something wild and untamed and a little scary. And then Sam looked away.

'Apparently so.'

She sucked in a breath and straightened her shoulders. At some point she'd have to tell him she was pregnant, but not here, not now, not like this, and if they were going to have this baby, at some point they would need to get to know each other. But, again, not now. Now

Kate had a job to do, and she was going to have to put her feelings on the back burner and resist the urge to run away.

Don't Miss
THEIR MEANT-TO-BE BABY
By Caroline Anderson

Available February 2017
www.millsandboon.co.uk

Copyright ©2017 by Caroline Anderson

Give a 12 month subscription to a friend today!

Call Customer Services
0844 844 1358*

or visit
millsandboon.co.uk/subscription

* This call will cost you 7 pence per minute plus your phone company's price per minute access charge.

MILLS & BOON®

Why shop at millsandboon.co.uk?

Each year, thousands of romance readers find their perfect read at millsandboon.co.uk. That's because we're passionate about bringing you the very best romantic fiction. Here are some of the advantages of shopping at www.millsandboon.co.uk:

- **Get new books first**—you'll be able to buy your favourite books one month before they hit the shops

- **Get exclusive discounts**—you'll also be able to buy our specially created monthly collections, with up to 50% off the RRP

- **Find your favourite authors**—latest news, interviews and new releases for all your favourite authors and series on our website, plus ideas for what to try next

- **Join in**—once you've bought your favourite books, don't forget to register with us to rate, review and join in the discussions

Visit **www.millsandboon.co.uk**
for all this and more today!

MILLS & BOON

Why shop at millsandboon.co.uk